Starchasers:

The Stars and The Seeds

By Kay Hawkins

Cover art by Leah Keeler

Starchasers: The Stars and The Seeds

Kay Hawkins

Published by Starchasers Press

Copyright 2020

First Edition

Hardcover: 978-1-989548-06-6

Paperback: 978-1-989548-05-9

Ebook: 978-1-989548-07-3

Other books by Kay Hawkins
Starchasers Novels:
The Stars Will Rise
The Stars Are Calling
A Home Among The Stars
The Stars and The Seeds

Short Stories:
10 Years: A Starchasers story
Ultimate Pot
Canterbury Road Trip
Get Him A Dime Bag!

Dedication

To Luke Maynard,
For your continuing support
and encouragement
are what keeps me going.

Chapter 1

Rushing through the doors of the hospital, Skyler stopped at the front desk. "What room is Sandy Roux in?"

The nurse turned her head away from the computer. "What's your relation to the patient?"

Skyler caught his breath. "I'm her son, Skyler Therris. She is having a baby. Someone texted me an hour ago, telling me that she was in labour." He pulled out his tablet and showed it to the nurse.

She typed in a few things on her computer. "Room 406, go down the hall and take the elevator to level 4 and turn to your right. She should be right there."

"Thank you." He made his way down the hall. Getting off the elevator, the first thing he saw was Charles staring right at him with a small bag of rippled chips in his hand.

"What are you doing here?" Charles took a chip out of the bag.

"My mother asked me to be here," said Skyler, "so I'm here. Is she in the room?"

He scanned Skyler with his eyes. "She also asked you to drop out of the academy, and by your lack of uniform, am I to assume you have started listening to her?"

Skyler shook his head. "Still there, just off duty. Sorry for the black t-shirt and blue jeans. What's with the suit?"

Charles finished his bag of chips. "I always wear a suit when in public and you should listen to you mother more, you'll live longer."

"Not if I stayed home with you, unless you forgot how many times you tried to kill me," Skyler said, making his way towards his mother's room.

Charles grabbed his arm and pulled him closer. "You listen to me now, I don't want you here and you might as well go back to space cadets."

Skyler furiously shook Charles's hand off him. "Don't you touch me again. I'm here because my mother asked me. Once the baby is born, I'm out of here and you don't have to see me again."

Charles narrowed his eyes at Skyler. "I don't think so. You have not been involved this entire time. What makes you think you have the right to be here?"

"That is my mother in that room," Skyler snapped back. With his arm stretched out he pointed to the room. "She is giving birth to my brother, your spawn, and I promised her I would be here and I am."

Charles grabbed Skyler's arm again pulling him towards the elevator. "You're a fuck-up and you have already broken your mother's heart, so don't come here and make things worse."

Skyler struggled with his arm. "I told you, don't touch me! You never did know what personal space meant!"

The elevator door opened and three reporters with press hats and tablets stepped off.

"You let go of my arm now, or I will tell the press what you have done to me."

Charles let go of Skyler's arm. Skyler rubbed his arm. *Damn, I think that is going to bruise.* He left Charles to talk to the reporters and went over to his mother's bedside. He saw his mother lying there on the bed in her hospital gown. Her eyes were half open and she was rubbing her belly.

Her eyes opened and a smile crossed her face. "Oh Skyler, you made it." She held out her hand for him to hold.

He took her hand and sat down next to her. "I said I would, even though I don't agree with this."

She brushed her hand on his face. "The baby is going to be born no matter what you do. You're finally going to be a big brother. You know I almost had a second child with your father."

Skyler took a deep breath and with a heavy heart replied: "Yes, I know. That is one thing you told me about you and Dad. But, why didn't you?"

A single tear ran down her face. "First it was because he refused unless we moved to space with him. The second time I said no because I found out about his stupid whore. But a few months before he died I changed my mind to give him a child next time I saw him." She paused and the tears flooded her eyes. "I never saw him again. I'm so sorry."

Skyler leaned over and gave his mother a hug. "You can't change it now, Mom. It wasn't meant to be."

She put her arms around Skyler. "Are you mad at me that Charles is the father?"

He backed off. "Honestly yes, I don't want this kid born but there is nothing I can do about it. I came because you wanted me here, not for this little brat."

She wiped the tears from her eyes. Her lips formed as if she was about to say something but let out a loud scream instead. She grabbed her belly. "Get the doctor! The baby is coming!"

Skyler jumped out of his seat and ran out to the hall. From the doorway, he called, "doctor, nurse, the baby is coming!" He rushed back into the room once he saw the nurse run down the hall. He sat there holding his mother's hand.

Charles entered the room and went to his wife's other side, holding her hand.

The nurse came in and checked the status of the baby. She looked at Skyler and Charles. "I'm going to get her to push in a second. You sure you both want to be here?"

Skyler nodded. "This is my mother and I promised I would be here. I can handle it." He scanned the room. He saw Charles glaring at him and the reporters were standing outside the door.

The doctor entered the room. He checked Sandy to make sure she was ready. "Okay Mrs. Roux I'm going to get you to push as hard as you can. On my count 1…2…3…Push!"

She crushed Skyler's hand as she pushed with all her might letting out a loud screech.

Skyler had been around a handful of pregnant women in his life but this was his first birth. He felt as if his hand was about to shatter in her grip. Every time the doctor said to push, her grip got tighter. He looked over at Charles who was putting a damp cloth on his wife's head. He glanced at Charles's hand, *Why isn't he complaining? My mom can't just be gripping my hand.*

The doctor called out "push" one more time and just when Skyler thought his hand would be busted for life, the baby came out.

The doctor pulled the baby out and Sandy let go of Skyler's hand. He rubbed his swollen red throbbing hand and watched Charles cut the cord. "It's a boy." The doctor handed the baby to the nurse to clean off.

The nurse returned the crying baby all wrapped in a blue blanket and handed it to Charles. A tear and a smile crossed his face. He kissed the baby boy on the forehead and handed him to his wife. Sandy held her baby boy and tickled his cheeks. "Phineas Adam Roux, that's your name, you little one. You're going to grow up big and strong and one day be President, yes you are." She turned her head up at Charles and said, "He looks so much like you."

Skyler, feeling uncomfortable now, defensively snarked. "Um you named him Penis? And president, really? You really want to start off his life with that kind of pressure?"

Charles glared at Skyler. "His name is Phineas, not penis. It was my father's name. He is my son and he will be president."

"Check the spelling of Phineas, take out the H and A and switch the E and I and you got penis. You got the future president Penis. I guess it's fitting since all you politicians are dicks." Skyler got up out of his chair.

"You listen to me, you little punk. Shut up now before I have you removed."

Sandy held up the baby. "Skyler, you want to hold him for a moment, just this once?"

Skyler let out a deep sigh and accepted the baby. He stared into the dark eyes of his new half-brother. He whispered quietly into his ear. "You're a cute little brat. Don't grow up like these two." He held onto him for a minute. When he was done, he handed the baby to the nurse, looking at his mother who was exhausted. "You get some rest, I got to go." He turned and walked out of the room.

Waiting for the elevator, he watched as Charles went out and talked to the press one more time. The elevator doors opened and out walked his Uncle Justin and Aunt Ruby. Skyler smiled.   "Hey Uncle Justin, you missed all the action."

Justin gave his nephew a hug. "It's great to see you here, and so what is it? She knew before, but didn't tell us."

Skyler hugged his uncle back and then his aunt. "It's a boy, Penis Adam Roux. 5lbs 9oz. He is definitely Charles's spawn."

Aunt Ruby frowned. "Penis? Skyler, be serious, did they really name him that?"

Skyler shook his head. "No, it's Phineas, but close enough."

Justin patted Skyler on the back. "You really are your father's son with that sense of humor. So, let me guess, they're both in there, right?"

Skyler looked behind him. "Charles is with that group of reporters and Mother is sleeping. I was just about to head out."

Justin gave his nephew one last hug. "Well in that case, we will wait here and see you later."

Skyler hit open on the elevator doors. "Ya, see you later." Once he walked out of the hospital, he picked up his phone and called Perry. "Hey buddy, any chance you want to go out for some drinks?"

"Skyler, it's three in the afternoon."

Skyler looked at the clock outside the hospital door. "Ya, so? we can go for happy hour specials, my treat?" he offered, making his way to his car as he talked.

Perry took a moment to respond. "Okay as long you're buying I guess I'm in. Meet you at the campus bar?"

Skyler got into his car. "Sounds good to me. See you in an hour."

Chapter 2

Skyler walked up to Perry who was sitting at the bar. "Sorry I made you wait. I was a distance away when I called."

Perry finished off his drink. "It's fine. I had some last-minute packing to do. Are you all packed?"

Skyler gave a signal to the bartender to bring them two beers. "Naw, I will finish packing tonight if I'm not drunk out of my mind. It's only the first, we leave on the third. I got time."

Perry patted Skyler on the back. "Are you excited to spend the year on Catillion?"

The bartender handed them their beers. Skyler took a large sip out of his. "Yup, I miss Michael and Kax. I hope they are enjoying their time."

Perry tilted his head. "Haven't you talked to them since they left?"

Skyler put his beer down. "A couple of times, but the time change and schedules make it hard. They have sent me a few photos. Kax is staying in the dorms and Michael has an officer's barracks."

Perry took a sip of his beer. "Yup, Michael is hard to get ahold of. I mostly just send him the files he needs and hear back from him much later. But two more days and we're going to be there."

Skyler finished his beer and waved for another one.

"So, what's wrong with you today?" Perry said, finishing his beer.

Skyler turned his head to Perry and laughed. "Um, what makes you think anything is wrong with me?"

Perry chuckled. "Dude, you're drinking in the middle of the afternoon and you're buying. There is no special occasion, you're slouching in your seat and going through those beers quite quickly."

Skyler exhaled. "My brother was born today. I just got back from the hospital."

Perry grinned. "Then we should be celebrating!"

Skyler drank his beer. "No, I don't want the little spawn. I promised my mother I would go to the birth and that's it. I hope I never have to see little Penis again."

Perry lowered his brow. "They named him Penis? And is he your only sibling? How far are you apart?"

"He's my half-brother," said Skyler, "and we're twenty-one years apart. His name's not Penis but it's close, Phineas Adam Roux. Phineas after Charles's father and Adam because he is Charles's first son. The little brat looks like Charles too. It will probably be in the paper tomorrow with all the details."

Perry took a sip of his beer. "Right, because Charles is a senator. Well, nothing you can do about it now. Let's drink to your little brother's health."

Skyler glared at Perry. "Get bent. I want to get drunk out of my mind and get laid. Forget this day ever happened." He chugged his newest beer and went over to a foxy redhead he saw sitting alone at one of the tables. "Hello miss, you alone? Would you care if I joined you at your table?"

The older woman smiled. "You can sit down, but what you going to do about your friend over there?"

Skyler waved Perry over. "Well if you got a friend, he won't be so lonely."

She shook Skyler's hand. "The name's Azibelle and you must be pretty lonely or upset to be picking up women in the middle of the afternoon."

"Let's avoid talking about me right now and let's focus on you."

Perry came over. "Perry, this is Azibelle." The two shook hands.

She rubbed her hand through Skyler's curly blonde hair. "Buy me a couple of drinks and we will see where it goes." She turned her attention to Perry. "Sorry I don't have a friend for you but I'm not against a threesome."

Perry's face went red and he turned his attention to Skyler.

Skyler shrugged. "A few more drinks and I will be willing to do just about anything."

Perry got an uneasy look across his face.

***

Morning, Perry got out of the bed putting his pants on. He walked over to where Skyler lay on the floor. He knelt and shook Skyler awake.

Skyler opened his bloodshot eyes. He rubbed his head. "Why is my head sore? Where am I? And did we have a threesome?"

Perry helped Skyler up. "You got too drunk and passed out on the floor. We're in my dorm, and yes we did."

Skyler sat on the empty bed in and rubbed his head. "There was another bed and you let me sleep on the floor?"

"You fell off the bed," Perry said, "and I, um, well, I kind of had my hands full. Sorry buddy." Hesitantly, he sat next to Skyler. "We got a little close last night. You were really drunk and acting weird."

Skyler let out a sigh and lay down on his bed. "Sorry if I made you feel weird yesterday was a strange day for me."

Perry laid down next to Skyler on the bed. "What is really eating you? There is more than your little brother that is upsetting you."

Skyler rolled away from Perry. "Lots of things, but the big one is this: it means my mother's marriage to that asshole is real. Even if he dies, there is evidence. Charles is horrible and I have no idea why she loves him and how she can stay with him. I can't change or stop any of this. I just want the brat gone, I want them all gone and out of my life. I don't want to kill my brother but I wish he was never created."

Concerned for his friend, Perry moved closer to Skyler and gave him a hug. "I'm sorry this is eating you up so badly. I love my little sister. But she is my full sister. I think it would bother me too if my mom remarried a guy who hated my guts and wanted more kids. But what can we do about these things?"

Skyler curled up into a little ball. "I have never had a say in any of this. She just did it and asked me about it later. I'm done with her. No more. I can't stand her and I'm not dealing with her no more."

"Did you tell them about going to Catillion for the year?"

Skyler shook his head. "I'm not telling them. I'm done with them. I only got me in this world. I like my aunt and uncle but that's it. You, Kax, Michael and Cane are my family now."

Perry hugged Skyler a little tighter. "Thanks for considering me family. Are we brothers?"

Skyler rolled back over and looked Perry straight in the eyes. "No." He chuckled, "you're more like an annoying cousin."

"Jerk!" He pushed Skyler away, knocking him onto the floor. Perry jumped off the bed to make sure Skyler was alright.

Skyler hit his head on the bed post. He sat up on the floor rubbing his head. "Damn it dude, you're going to give me a concussion!"

Perry sat back down on the bed. "I'm sorry. That's not what I intended."

Skyler got up and looked at his bump in the mirror. "Come on, Perry, let's go to my room. I need to pack."

"I thought you said you still have time," Perry offered, but Skyler was already moving.

Chapter 3

Kax kissed the older man underneath her. She rubbed her hands through his greying brown hair. She moved down, kissing his neck and bare chest. Moving her hips up, things were just about to get hot and heavy when in the background a musical chime could be heard. She leaned over and grabbed her phone out of her jacket pocket and looked at the time. Her eyes widened. "I'm so sorry, Kreeve, I got to go. My friends' shuttle is arriving, and we're all supposed to meet for drinks. We haven't seen each other all summer." She got off his lap, stood up and zipped up her cadet uniform.

He sat up on the couch, putting his hands around her hips and pulling her back down. He kissed her neck and fondled her breasts. "Come on, we have time for a quickie. You're a pilot, you know shuttles never arrive on time."

She purred at his touch. She turned and played with his brown catlike ears. "I know, but still I should be there. Don't worry, I won't forget about you. I'll make it up to you tomorrow. You can do whatever you want to me."

A big grin crossed his face and he grabbed her ass and whispered into her ear. "Even that?"

She hesitantly smiled and gave him a kiss. "Even that." She fixed up her hair and got up off the couch. "See you tomorrow."

***

Michael's alarm on his work desk went off. He closed his books and stood up. "Dr. Fogg, I got to go. My friends' shuttle is arriving."

Dr. Fogg picked his head up from looking in one of the potted plants. "Sounds good to me, just be back here at 6 a.m. sharp. We need to check on the plants and there should be enough sunlight out at that time."

Michael took off his lab coat and put on his brown leather jacket. "No problem. I might have a bit of a hangover but I will be here."

Dr. Fogg got up and walked over to Michael and gave him a pat on the back. "You have fun tonight, you need the break. I have not had an apprentice who works as hard as you in years. Do all Squallites work as hard as you?"

"No, I think it is just me." Michael smiled. "Am I that good?"

Dr. Fogg shook his head. "No, that's a bad thing. Lighten up. Even the plants are more active than you."

Michael looked down at his feet. "So 6 a.m. tomorrow, I will be here."

Dr. Fogg patted Michael on the back. "I know you will. Go out and try to have fun."

Michael made his way down to the docking bay. He went up to the crowded platform. He checked his tablet for the time and to make sure he had the right location, when two hands covered his eyes from behind.

"Guess who, tall stuff," said a sweet feminine voice.

Turning around, he picked her up in a hug. "Kax, there you are. I am so happy to see you."

Kax's catlike ears wiggled as she hugged Michael back. "It's been a while. I guess our schedules have just been busy."

Michael put Kax down. "Maybe my boss is right. I do need to get out more."

She poked his chest. "You're fine just the way you are."

His face went red. "Speaking of things that never change, Skyler's shuttle seems to be a bit late."

Kax let out a sigh. "Yeah, they're never on time. But once he is here, you're never going to get rid of him."

Oh dear, I forgot about how clingy Skyler can be. I hope I will have time for work and him. He brushed off the comment. "I guess you are right. Maybe it was a good idea spending the summer away from him."

Kax looked down at her feet. "As much as I have enjoyed the summer without him, I do feel bad we left him on Earth alone."

"What do you mean 'alone?' Perry was there to keep him company."

Bells started to ring as the shuttle started to dock. Michael and Kax rushed with the crowd to the doors of the shuttle. There were security guards keeping the people back for safety reasons.

The ship landed and the doors opened. Skyler and Perry walked out of the shuttle with a crowd of people.

Michael waved to them, getting their attention. Skyler and Perry made their way over to Michael and Kax. Skyler pushed his way through the crowd. He made his way to Kax, putting his hands on her shoulders, pulling her close and hugged her tightly. He kissed her passionately. He broke the kiss and gazed into her golden cat eyes. "I have missed you, and waited all summer to kiss you."

She made a fist but then smiled. "Oh Skyler, you lovable jerk."

He grinned and brushed her hair back. "You willing to give me a chance this year?"

She turned her head away from Skyler. "I'm sorry, Skyler. I—"

"Don't worry about it," said Skyler. He turned his attention to Michael. "So did you find us a good bar to go to?"

Michael shook his head. "Sorry, I have been working. I have not been to a single bar or had a drink all summer. Do you not have to get your room assignment and put your stuff away?"

Skyler looked over at Perry and shook his head. "Naw, we will just put our bags in the car. Me and Perry already know we're roommates."

"Well, in that case…" Michael looked over at Kax. "Do you know any good bars?"

She nodded. "Yup, there's one that my sister goes to all time, the Sandbox. I have been there once before."

Skyler grinned. "Well then let's get going."

Chapter 4

Early in the morning Michael only got two hours of rest before he had to get up and move the plants. He got dressed and made his way to the lab.

Dr. Fogg had the plants all packaged up and ready to go. "6 a.m. sharp, you're so reliable."

Michael rubbed his head before picking up one of the trays of plants. "I got two hours of rest, but it was still nice to get caught up with friends."

Dr. Fogg walked up to Michael and placed a bag into his hand. He looked at Michael's eyes. "Huh, never seen a Squallite with bloodshot eyes before. It's kind of cute."

Michael rolled his eyes. "Is every doctor I work with going to have a crush on me?"

Dr. Fogg patted Michael on the back and laughed. "I'm not interested in you like that. Just the orange bloodshot eyes remind me of tiger lilies and people will find that cute. Women love flowers, especially lilies. Have you thought about getting a girlfriend?"

Michael headed to the door. "I have thought of it. But it is just not the time for me."

Dr. Fogg opened the door before picking up a tray. "Too bad. You're a smart, talented, hardworking guy, you deserve someone who will watch out for you when you have been working twelve hours straight. Then keep you warm at night when you finally decide to sleep."

Michael made his way to the roof of the building. "You sure there is going to be sunlight today? It seems pretty dark." He placed the tray of plants down.

Dr. Fogg looked at the sky. "Yup it will be here. I have lived on this planet for six years now. I can tell you the sun cycles better than the weather men." He placed his tray down.

Michael opened the bag and set up the solar collector tripod.

Dr. Fogg watched him as he worked. "So tell me about last night? What happened?"

Michael tightened the stand of the tripod. "Well, me, Skyler, Perry and Kax went to this bar called the Sandbox. It was our first time there and it was like something you would see on Earth: hard wood floors, wood paneling on the walls, dim lights. Nothing like the rest of the architecture you see anywhere else here. You have no idea how much stairs on the walls and low ceilings bother me. It was nice to be in what I would call a normal building."

Dr. Fogg laughed. "You get used to it, but you're taller than me by five inches so it might take you a bit more time. What else happened?"

Michael started setting up the other tripod. "Well, Skyler and Perry tried to drag me into a drinking contest. I got five beers in before I got sick and went back to something light. Skyler tried to score with Kax and she turned him down so he found another girl and left with her. Perry also tried to pick up a girl and failed. We all just had a good time getting caught up, it was really nice seeing them again."

"That's really great to hear but your eyes are that red after five beers? You really are a lightweight. I'm glad you had fun with your friends. If you ever need time off, let me know and you can have it you've earned it. I'm also looking forward to working with Perry in a few days. The solar energy we collected was a big help. I just hope this time we got the genes right so we can work on improving them and not just growing. We need results."

Michael checked the plants one more time, making sure they were all healthy. "These plants are ready to go."

Dr. Fogg checked his watch. "Okay, Michael, step back here with me. We want the plants to get all the light they can."

They sat back in the fold-out chairs they had set up and watched how the asteroid field shifted and let through a large burst of sunlight. Michael covered his face from the light.

Dr. Fogg handed Michael a pair of sunglasses. "After two weeks of darkness the sun can be quite bright."

Michael put the glasses on. "You get so used to darkness and then bam, light. I know Catillions have better eyes for this but I have no idea if I will be able to go back to Earth when this is over with the whole night and day."

"It's not that bad, Michael. You just have bloodshot eyes so it makes it worse. If you want to wait inside, you can. I will call you when the plants are done. I just want to get some sun."

Michael looked at the plants. "Naw, I can wait for the plants to be done. A little sunlight will not hurt me."

Three hours later the asteroid cloud came back over and the darkness returned. Michael got up and took down the solar collectors. "When is the next burst of sunlight due?"

Dr. Fogg looked at his watch. "There is going to be one at midnight, and then the next one after that is a week from tomorrow. You don't have to come back tonight. The amount of sun collected from these solar collectors today should give these plants about three months of pure sunlight." He handed the tray of plants to Michael. "If you need to sleep you can go home. I didn't think you would be this tired."

Michael carried the tray back to the lab. "Squallites meditate, we do not sleep, and I can stay for the day. We got the sunlight and we need to convert it and redistribute it. It is a big job for you to do alone."

"You really know how to overwork yourself." He put his tray back into its container. "Well then, we got work to do."

***

Ouch. My head hurts. Where am I? Skyler scanned the strange orange-painted room with an odd round door. *Why is it round? Where am I?*

The door opened. Perry walked into the room. He was wearing a towel on his waist and drying his hair with another. "Hey, roomie. You got to try the showers here, you will love them. The water is blue."

Skyler rubbed his eyes. "Perry, where am I?"

Perry grabbed his uniform out of the closet. "I told you to stop drinking. Do you remember the girl you came back with last night?"

Rubbing his temples, Skyler watched Perry get dressed. "We're on Catillion. It is all coming back to me now. The girl left at like 3 a.m. and I passed out. And I won the drinking contest."

Perry stood over in the corner of the room with his back to Skyler and got changed. "I'm very surprised that you were able to perform. You had so much alcohol in you I was worried you were going to die or something. Don't drink that much again. Catillion beer is different." Perry turned around after getting dressed.

Skyler got out of bed, exposing himself to Perry.

Perry coughed.

Skyler looked down and grabbed the blanket off the bed to cover himself, "I should have guessed I was naked." He searched the floor with his eyes. "Where are my clothes?"

Perry walked over to the end of Skyler's bed and picked the clothes off the floor. "These are what you were wearing last night but we have class at noon so you want your uniform." He walked over to the closet and pulled out Skyler's uniform.

Skyler took the uniform and looked at the window. "It's nighttime. Are you sure class is so soon?"

Perry pulled up a sun schedule on his tablet and showed Skyler. "See, there is an asteroid field that blocks the light to the planet. It moves and then we get sunlight. You missed the sun this morning, it was out for about two hours. Very hot."

Skyler started putting his uniform on. "How much time do we have before class?"

Perry looked at the clock. "I would say a good hour. Why is there something you wanted to do?"

Skyler zipped up his cadet jacket. "Ya, I want to stop by Kax's room and see how she's doing."

Perry unzipped a pouch in his suitcase. "Okay, but first take one of these." He handed Skyler a little orange pill. "You're going to need that hangover cure for your first day."

Skyler swallowed the pill. "Okay then, let's get going to Kax's dorm."

***

Kax was brushing her reddish brown hair in front of her mirror when she heard the knock at the door. She unzipped her uniform top. She sat on her bed with her legs open. "Come in." She called.

Skyler and Perry entered the room.

Skyler grinned. "Well now that's the best greeting I have ever received from you."

Eyes popping, she zipped up her top and crossed her legs. "Skyler! Perry! What are you doing here?"

Skyler checked Kax out with a grin. "You're not wearing your leggings. Who were you expecting before class?"

She tried to pull down her skirt. "My boyfriend sometimes stops in before class. It is getting late for him so he probably isn't stopping by. What are you two doing here, anyway?"

Perry scanned the room. "You have this room to yourself? Nice."

"Stop staring at my legs, Skyler!" She reached over and grabbed her leggings off her chair. "Yes, all of us deep space cadets have private rooms. Could you boys turn around while I put on my leggings?"

The two boys turned away from Kax.

"Since when do you have a boyfriend?" Skyler tried to turn his head. "What does he have that I don't?"

She put her leggings on one leg at a time. "I have had one for most of this summer. As for what he has, it's more of what he isn't. He is very mature and stable in his work. He's not like you, king of the one-night stands." She finished putting her leggings on. "You can turn around now."

Perry sat down on the bed next to Kax. He looked at her with big puppy dog eyes. "Could I be your boyfriend?"

Kax leaned over and looked Perry in the eyes. "You're cute, Perry, and one day you will make a girl very happy, but you're not my type. You're more like a cute little brother."

Skyler sat on the other side of Kax.

She turned to look at him and could see the hurt look on his face. She put her arm around him. "You and me, Skyler, are just friends. You sleep with other girls. I'm sleeping with another man. No difference."

He let out a heavy sigh. He got up off the bed and walked out the door.

Perry looked at Kax. "I will go talk to him. Nice seeing you again. I hope it works out with you and your boyfriend. Maybe we can double date sometime, when I find a girlfriend." He got off the bed and left the room.

***

Perry rushed after Skyler who was speeding down the hall, and caught up with him in the courtyard. "Skyler, stop running and talk to me. I know you are upset, but who knows? This relationship may not even work."

Skyler turned around and stared dead into Perry's eyes. "Kax is the love of my life! Her with another man, I can't imagine it. What's wrong with me?"

Perry's eyes went sad. "I don't know, maybe cut back on the girls. Maybe find a way to prove you're stable and ready to move on to something more serious. You heard her. She wants a mature guy. Could it really hurt to try and cut back on the drinking and women and study a bit more?"

Skyler groaned. "Drinking I can do. Women will be hard and you know why. Studying, do I have to? It is so hard for me to study. I read it all when I was a kid. I know my stuff, I have my dad's textbooks and log files. Reading these textbooks now is so mundane."

"Okay then, just take school more serious. And maybe get a girlfriend, someone really serious, show her you can make a commitment and stick with it."

Skyler sat down on the bench next to them. "Perry, just leave me alone, okay? I need time to think. This is not the first time. But this is the first time Kax has taken this long to tell me she has been with someone. I'm trying to just process this. Leave me alone and I'll see you in the dorm later."

With remorse, he looked down at his friend. "I will see you at the dorm."

***

Skyler sat on the bench, leaning back staring at the clouds. The darkness of the sky made him feel peaceful there was a new set of stars for him to memorize. His chest was heavy. *Why does she play with my heart like this so much?*

"Hey hot stuff, I'm lost. Could you help me with directions?" A feminine voice said.

He picked up his head and turned towards the voice. He saw a black-haired woman with purple streaks, hazel cat eyes and black catlike ears smiling at him. "By your lack of a uniform, I assume you're not a cadet. I'm new here, so I don't know my way around, but I could do my best to help you."

She sat down next to Skyler on the bench and pulled out her map. "See I'm trying to get to the deep space training barracks right now to visit my sister, but I'm not sure how to get there from here."

Skyler didn't even look at the map. He pointed to the side. "They're right there, you found them. But they're all in class about now. Where I should be."

The girl held out her hand. "My name's Kandice. Why aren't you in class?"

He shook her hand. "Skyler. I just found out this girl I like has a boyfriend. I don't feel much like learning today."

"I hope you are feeling like learning tomorrow." She said, "don't let a girl keep you down for long. Guys who study are hot."

The spark in his eyes returned. "We could go to the study hall and you could watch me sit there with my nose in a book if that's what you're into?"

She placed her hand on his knee. "We could do that, or go to the campus bar I have been meaning to try."

Skyler put on a charming smile. "Do you always go up to random guys on benches and take them out for drinks?"

She played with one of the curls on his head. "No, you just looked like you could use some cheering up."

He stood up. "Well, in that case, let's go to the bar."

She got up and took his arm. "Well then, cutie, let's get going. I bet I can drink you under the table and wash that sorrow away."

Skyler laughed and shook his head. "No drinking contests tonight. I had one last night with friends and my liver hasn't recovered. Also if things heat up tonight I prefer not to black out in the middle."

In the light of the bar he could see her face more clearly. He placed his hand on her cheek. "I love your cheekbones they're so strong. And your hair, is that natural?"

She took a sip of her drink. "100%, I got my dad's cheekbones. They look better on me in my opinion."

He held her hand. "I think you have a very feminine face. A very lovely one at that."

She reached out and touched his ear. "You're the cutest human I have ever seen. I love these little pink skin ears, are so soft. Not what I would imagine they felt like."

Skyler flinched at her touch. "Stop that. It tickles. Have you even been with a human before?"

She shook her head. "Considering I did live on Earth for most of my life I never did. I did always find them cute. I like your ears but there are so many other aliens on Earth it's hard to date them all."

Skyler looked confused. "So, you collect men?"

She laughed. "Not really. I find Catillions boring. And there's so many interesting things about other aliens. I want to try them out and see what is so different." As she talked her tails curled up.

Skyler looked behind her. "You have two tails? Shouldn't you have only one?"

She smiled, moving her tails forward. "I have two, one black and one blonde. One is my brother's tail. He is in a wheelchair and they were going to have to remove it. And I wanted to feel closer to him so I took it."

"That's a bit odd, but okay." Skyler took a sip of his beer and scanned around the room. "Isn't there a cure for your brother? Hey, why do some of you have tails and others don't?"

"He was born with a deformed spine and Catillions have a very complicated nervous system in the spine. It's inoperable." She took a sip of her drink. "Evolution. We used to all have tails but over the generations, fewer and fewer do. My mom had a tail and my dad didn't. So, me and my brother have tails but my sister doesn't."

Skyler accepted that answer. "Well I have never been with a Catillion with a tail. It looks very sexy, especially since you have two."

"I guess it will be a first for both of us."

"I must admit I'm not used to girls picking me up like this and then buying me drinks. Have had a couple but not a lot. But I don't mind a fling with you."

She played with her straw in her drink. "Well, if you're good, I was hoping for something a bit more..."

He raised an eyebrow. "What exactly are you thinking?"

She sipped from her straw. "I was hoping if this goes well, we could be friends with benefits. I have gone too long without someone and looking for someone new but I don't want a boyfriend or to be tied down."

Skyler contemplated it for a moment. "I wouldn't mind something regular. New planet. New places. It would be nice to have someone show me some new things. So I guess if you're clean and we have a good time together, then why not?"

She finished her drink and leaned in to kiss Skyler on the lips. "And if that girl you like becomes single and we're together, don't worry, you can be with her. I won't mind considering this arrangement as very casual. I will probably drop you before you can drop me, though. Life is too short to stay with one person forever."

Wow that was an awesome kiss. He grinned with delight. "Are all you Catillions like this? Or am I just lucky?"

"We're a bit more open when it comes to sex. Finding partners is easy for us but this is your lucky day." She brushed her hand through his hair. "I love your cute curls."

Skyler brushed his hair with his hand. "I hate my curls. I wish I had straight hair but at least they're not tight curls, just a wave. I would really hate tight curls."

She laughed. "You're so cute."

He finished his beer. "Well someone has to like them. I guess it better be the ladies."

She looked right into his eyes. "So if you're skipping classes does that mean your roommate's out and we have the room to ourselves?"

Skyler pulled out his wallet and put the money for the drinks on the table. "Ya, my roommate is in class but even if he was at the room he wouldn't mind. He is used to me."

She picked up his money off the table and paid for the drinks. "Earth money is no good here, you will need to get it converted. Remember I said would cover the drinks. I did ask you out."

Skyler put his wallet away, "Oh right, sorry, just a habit, thank you."

"Come on, let's go have some fun," she whispered in his ear.

Chapter 5

Skyler lay awake in his bed. Kandice was by his side. He kissed her neck. "Thanks for spending the night with me again."

She purred with delight. "Well I drove all the way out here. I think I'm going to stay, plus I like that you're a cuddler."

He kissed her lips passionately.

The door opened and the sound of a throat clearing caught Skyler's attention. He looked at the door and saw Perry standing there with a towel.

"Skyler, is she still here?" He said drying his hair.

Skyler laughed. "She was just leaving. We got class today." He turned and looked at Kandice. "I'm sorry, Kandy, I got to go learn some things."

She got out of bed and started getting dressed.

Michael walked into the room. "Um did I miss something? I feel a bit overdressed."

Skyler laughed. "Nice to see you again, buddy. What's up?"

Michael turned away and looked at the wall while they got dressed. "I am here to pick up Perry for work, and Skyler, I think we are going to need you too. We are testing some plants and Perry was to start today and I know you do not like going to class anyway, Skyler."

Perry's eyes lit up. "I can't wait to work on our plants, this is going to be rad!"

Kandice kissed Skyler one more time. "I'm going to go visit my sister before she has to get to class, so I will see you later. Enjoy your botany lesson."

Skyler waved goodbye and got dressed. "Okay, I will help you but I want class credit for it."

Michael rubbed his temples. "You got to talk to Dr. Fogg about that, but since when have you cared?"

Skyler combed his hair. "Since I got here. I have been taking class much more seriously. Also, you can turn around, we're all dressed now."

Perry nodded his head. "He's right. Except for the first day he has not missed a single day of class, even if it's only been a week."

Michael turned around. "Well I am impressed. Maybe this new girl is good for you? Or was she a girl of the night?"

Skyler flung his comb onto his bed. "We're friends with benefits. She's not a cadet. We met because her sister is a pilot."

Michael shifted his eyes. "Who is her sister?"

Skyler scratched his head. "No idea, never asked. We have just been getting to know each other."

Perry put on his backpack. "I got my kit ready. Let's go play with some plants."

***

Kandice opened the door. "Hey sis, how are you doing?"

Kax was brushing her hair. "Hey sis, how have you been? You have been coming by less and less, did you meet someone?"

Kandice sat down on the bed. "Yup he is this cute human guy. My first human boy and he is talented."

Kax sat next to her sister on the bed. "Well I'm glad you are happy."

Kandice grinned. "You should try him out. The things he can do with his tongue." She purred. "It's like magic. I might just keep this one."

Kax laughed. "I never thought you would settle down. Especially with a human."

Kandice laughed, tossing her hair. "No, marriage is out of the question. He wants to be a captain and I would be willing to travel with him but only as a captain's girl. He is just a buddy."

Kax shook her head. "Sis, your sex life confuses me."

Kandice laughed. "Believe me, when this guy goes down on you, you can see stars. He is not one you want to let go of. Is your boyfriend that good?"

Kax looked down at her feet. "No, he is not that good but he is strong, big and knows how to handle a woman."

Kandice rolled her eyes. "He's old, what do you expect? If he doesn't know what to do with a woman I would be worried. Any guy knows where to put it, but how to use it is another story."

Kax's face turned red. "I'm content with my love life. He may not make me see stars but I bet yours is a young immature guy who is reckless and has a big ego."

"I will never understand your fascination with old men. Sure, they're mature, but most of them are married or just wanting a young play toy. I would rather do it with a young guy and give him some practice."

There was a knock at the door. Kandice got off the bed and answered the door. An older mature Catillion man was standing on the other side.

"Hello, who are you?" The man said looking at Kandice.

She smiled. "Kax is my sister, and you must be the boyfriend." She looked back at Kax, "He really is old."

Kax got off the bed and pushed her sister aside and let him in. "Sorry about my sister. She likes immature guys and doesn't know what a real man is like."

He leaned in and kissed her on the lips. "That is her problem, but I'm glad you like me."

Kax batted her eyelashes at him. She turned to her sister. "Kandice, this is my boyfriend, Commodore Kreeve."

Kandice held out her hand. "Nice to meet you. Just letting you know if you hurt my sister, I will cut off your dick."

He shook her hand. "I don't do anything to your sister that she doesn't want."

Kax kissed Kreeve one more time. "Sis, I think it is time for you to leave. We're going to have fun before class."

Kandice headed to the door. "Well at least you're getting laid even if this guy is older than dad."

***

Skyler entered the lab and looked at the plants in the trays, and growing on the walls. "Is this a lab or a grow house?"

Michael walked in behind him. "It is both. We grow and study the plants. Each section has a different breed or a different treatment."

Perry stepped into the room, his jaw dropping in astonishment. "Oh my, I have not seen so many plants in years." His eyes wide, he looked at Michael. "Can't wait to be working here all year!"

"If you do a good job today here, Cadet Zyrix, I can put in a request for you to be here much longer than a year." Dr. Fogg held out his hand. "Dr. Fogg. It is nice to meet you boys."

Skyler shook his hand. "Am I going to get class credit for helping you with this?"

Dr. Fogg laughed. "You will get more than that if you want. Just do the work today and we will see where it goes."

Skyler stared at him with suspicion. "What kind of work are we doing today?"

Dr. Fogg grinned. "Follow me." He went to the far back of the room to the end of all the plants. "These plants are Michael's creation. Well I helped but it was his theory. They are Hydroponic projectile plant guns. Cross-bred with beans and the hyzuku plant and a few other things in there. But we think we have finally got this figured out. These plants can be weapons, rations and fertilizer for making new plants. These can easily be grown on ships and only take six days to grow.

Your ship would never have to carry crates of guns again. Your friend here is a genius."

Perry looked at Michael with his wide eyes. "You really are. This is great! Can you teach me everything you know? I love plants."

Michael turned his head and blushed. "It was just a theory. Dr. Fogg did all the work."

Skyler spoke up, "okay this is all nice and impressive but I want to know why you need us to help you?"

Dr. Fogg smiled. "Well it is like this," he waved his hands as he talked. "There are not many who know about this project and Michael said he could trust you. I need to see if I can trust you myself. I will give you both a plant and you will take care of it. Don't let it die. But what we are going to do today is test these plants in multiple climates."

Skyler frowned. "You two are the botanists. Shouldn't you be doing that?"

Dr. Fogg shrugged. "Yes but there are two of us and I have four climate rooms, fifty-two climate controls and 400 plants. The quicker we can get this done the sooner we can move to the next step."

Skyler turned around heading to the door. "Sorry doc, no sale. I want to be a captain not a scientist. Find someone else. I thought this would be more interesting."

Michael whispered to Dr. Fogg, "Do not worry; he is on board. He is just playing hard to get." Michael grabbed Skyler's shoulder and turned him around. "Come on buddy you know you want to help."

Skyler sighed and conceded. "Ya, I guess you're right."

Dr. Fogg went up to Skyler, placing his one hand on his shoulder and taking him away from the others. "Why I need you is you're a future captain. One day these will be on your ship. You will need to know how to care about them and what work goes into them. Also, when we test these out, we will be using the simulator and you will be calling all the shots. By doing this before the weapons are approved, you can consider this as extra credit and training before anyone else gets it. So, when the fleet admirals add these plants to the training and you have graduated, you won't have to worry about having to go back and learn. You will have it and you can train your crew." He put his other hand on Skyler's shoulder and stared into his eyes. "So, sound like fun?"

Skyler thought about it for a moment. "When you put it that way…if it gets me a promotion sooner, I don't mind pruning a few leaves."

Dr. Fogg gave Skyler a pat on the back. "You will still have to do your regular classwork. This will just count as extra credit and will probably take up more of your time."

Skyler shrugged. "Meh, I only get about four hours of sleep a night. I can handle this."

Perry was standing by the gardening shears. "Can I start cutting all the dead leaves off your plants?"

Dr. Fogg went over to Perry and took the pruners out of his hand. "Don't be too eager. You can do that tonight after the climate checks."

Michael picked up a small potted plant. "If everyone will please grab a plant and follow me, I will show you to your climate rooms."

They walked to the far wall of the building, where they saw four soundbooth-like rooms.

"You will take your plant, place it in the center of the room on that stool. Then each room has already been assigned your climates to test. Set the dial to the correct setting, then watch the plant and what happens. Leave each plant in there for no less than ten minutes. If you see some form of change, keep it in there longer. Document all that you see. Understood?"

Perry had already placed his plant in and was sitting down on his stool outside. "Ready to start."

Dr. Fogg put his hand on Perry's shoulder. "You are more eager to work than Michael. I just hope you get out more than him."

Skyler laughed. "He gets out alright, and will until the day I kill him with alcohol poisoning."

Perry burst out with laughter. "You drink more than me. You're the one who should be worried."

"You're a lightweight, that's why. I can handle my alcohol." Skyler gave Perry a high five.

Michael groaned. "Both of you will be dead before graduation if you keep drinking like you do."

Skyler rolled his eyes. "You sweat out the alcohol having sex. You would know that if you had some."

Dr. Fogg laughed, "I love this energy you boys have together. Reminds me of when I was a young lad."

Michael turned his head and continued with his work.

Dr. Fogg was sitting next to him and turned in his seat. "You know, Michael, we're not picking on you. You don't have to drink or have sex just to have fun. You give that job to Skyler."

Skyler smiled with pride. "Michael you know I have never had a problem doing enough girls for the both of us."

Perry shook his head. "Now you're going to have to give the girls to me, having a girlfriend and all."

Skyler brushed it off. "Kandy is no big deal, it's a casual thing. Who knows how long we will last? But I will make sure you get laid."

Dr. Fogg raised an eyebrow at Skyler. "Skyler is this girl Kandy a Catillion by any chance?"

Skyler nodded. "Ya, she picked me up which I found odd but she said it was normal here."

"It is normal for the women here to be more open to sex but I hope you are using condoms. They often do it because they want kittens. They find a guy they like for their DNA, get pregnant, take off and marry someone else. Not all Catillions do it, but usually the horny ones do."

Skyler swallowed and his hand shook. "Really? Well, I must watch out for that. I always use a condom, but I guess I'm going to stock up."

Perry looked at his plant and turned off the climate control and wrote something in his notebook. "No effect on the wasteland environment. Dr. Fogg, do you want me to use the same plant if there was no effect?"

He shook his head. "No, just in case there are any long-term effects, which we will look for on another day. Just mark on the tag which one it was under and grab another plant."

Perry got off his seat and got himself another plant.

Skyler looked at his, which he had forgotten to pay attention to. "Um, sir? I got the desert environment and mine's leaves are starting to dry out. Should I continue watching or take it out?"

"That is a reaction to the environment. Keep going and see what happens until the plant dies."

Michael's jaw dropped. "Until it dies? These plants are my babies, you cannot just kill them in the name of science!"

Dr. Fogg nodded his head. "Michael, I know how you feel. I was like that with my plants for the longest time. But if we don't let it die, how will we know how long it will last in the environment and what it does to the pods? You have to be willing to lose a couple in the name of science for more to grow more efficiently."

Michael got off his stool and looked in the window at Skyler's plant. He watched the two-foot plant he had bred, engineered and grown from a seedling start to shrivel and die. A tear rolled down his face.

Dr. Fogg gave him a moment. "Okay, Michael, you got to check on your plant now. I'm sorry about your plant but it was necessary and we will be lucky if it is the only one we lose today."

Michael wiped the tear off his face and went and sat down at his booth and watched his plant sit there and do nothing.

The hours passed. Some plants lived, some died, some thrived. Perry let out a loud yawn.

Dr. Fogg turned in his chair. "Perry you have done a good job today. You can go home. There are only about 30 minutes before I was going to tell you to break for dinner, but if you're tired, go back to your dorm and rest. Tomorrow is Saturday. We can get back to work on this then."

Skyler turned in his seat. "Wait, we have to come in on our weekends?"

"I'm sorry, but we need to get this work done. The war is getting more intense and they want all the weapons as soon as they can from all their sources. You won't have to work long on weekends, just a regular day, but if you're going to be doing this in your spare time your free time is going to be cut down."

Skyler rubbed his head. "This is going to be horrible. My social life is going to die."

Dr. Fogg laughed. "You said you only sleep four hours a night. If you work here until nine I think you still have time for one. If you don't want to continue this work you don't have to but like I told you before this is extra credit to get you one step closer to being a captain. If you don't want it, that is fine."

Well I have Kandice, and Kax is busy and the guys are here. There will be time for a social life when I become a captain. He nodded his head. "Deal. I got a steady girl so I won't have to go out looking. And hey I got you dudes to talk to. I can do this."

Dr. Fogg got off his chair and turned off his climate controller. "Sounds good to me. See you boys back here at 6 a.m. Pack a lunch."

Chapter 6

The lunch bell rang and Kax packed her books and got out of her seat. The other students were leaving and she followed behind them.

"Cadet Tillion," Commodore Kreeve asked, "could you please stay after class today?"

Kax turned around and made her way to the desk.

He gave her a devilish smile. "I'm sorry I have been busy this past week. I hope you will forgive me for not coming to visit you."

She put her books down on his solid wood desk. "Well I have missed you, but I think I can forgive you if you visit me tonight."

He stood up in front of her, leaning in to kiss her. "I think I can work that out. But in case I don't make it…" He caressed her butt gently. "I could give you a little treat now."

She looked back at the door and saw the window on the door. "We can't do it here. What if somebody sees us?"

He kissed her neck. "Don't worry. I have a plan. Get under the desk."

She looked at the desk. "Uh there is not enough room for both of us to fit under there."

"Just get under there." He slapped her ass.

She crawled into the open space under the desk.

He sat down in his chair and unzipped his pants.

***

A week of hard work getting the plants ready was wearing Skyler out. *So glad Dr. Fogg gave me lunch hour off. If I must eat my lunch next to another plant…ugh, I don't even want to think it.* He walked down the golden painted hallway. *I should see if Kax is around. I haven't seen her much but she has to have lunchtime off.*

He continued down the hall to her class door and looked in through the round window in the round door. His eyes bulged, his jaw dropped and his heart stopped. He stood there frozen watching Kax under the table. *No that can't be her, she wouldn't do that, not with him. Please let this be a dream.* He closed his eyes and opened them up a second later. He saw the same thing. He turned around, put his back to the wall and slid down. His heart was racing, *Oh my, that makes me want to throw up. My stomach hurts and my eyes need bleach. This is insane. Kax is a good girl, not the kind who gives their teachers blowjobs under their desk.*

He sat there for a few moments. Scared to stay but too scared to run away. He got the courage to stand up. He was about to walk away when the door next to him opened. His heart stopped. Time froze.

Kax came walking out of the room looking like nothing had happened. She turned and saw Skyler. "Hey, what you doing here?"

Skyler took a deep breath and smiled. "I got lunch off and was going to check and see if you wanted to go to lunch."

She smiled. "You know what, that sounds like a good idea."

Skyler and Kax headed down the hall.

"So, you have been here almost two weeks and I haven't seen you much. What is going on?"

Skyler tried to keep cool, but his chest was pounding. "I'm taking an extra credit course so I have been getting up early and going to bed late. No time for a social life. I have thought about stopping by to visit you, but I looked at the copy of the schedule you sent me and well I can't seem to find a time when you're awake. Are you doing anything tonight? Maybe we could go out or something with Michael, like old times."

She could tell something was bothering Skyler. "I'm sorry, I have a date tonight."

Skyler clenched his fist. He wanted to say something, but not in public. He turned right in the hall instead of left to the cafeteria.

Kax frowned. "Skyler, the cafeteria is back that way. Why are we going this way?"

He kept moving forward. "I forgot something in my room. I just need to get it before I can go for lunch. Don't worry, I'll be quick."

They got to the room and he closed the door, standing in front of it. He glared at Kax. "I'm going to be as calm as I can be about this and please don't lie to me."

She looked puzzled. "What are you talking about, Skyler?"

He took a deep breath, not breaking eye contact. "Who is your boyfriend?"

She took a deep breath and sat down on his bed. "If I tell, you can't tell anybody, okay? Not even Michael."

Skyler shook his head. "If he is who I think he is then I have to tell somebody. And if I tell Michael, that will be the least of your worries."

She looked down at her feet and covered her face. "Okay, it's Commodore Kreeve."

He shook his head, clenching his fist. "Kax he's your flight instructor. That's illegal, and he is in his 40s. Kax, I don't even date women that old."

She shook her head. "If I already graduated, we would be allowed to date. And he's in his 60s. Catillions age slower."

Skyler flung his hands in the air and pulled at his hair. "Kax, if you were graduated, he would not be your flight instructor. That's why it would be legal. Kax, why are you with him? You're not stupid. You know this can get you kicked out and you will lose everything. Is he really worth it?"

She shook her head. "Skyler, you just don't get it. He is a great guy and cares about me."

Skyler walked over and looked Kax in the eye. "Kax, please answer me these questions. How much do you care about him, and what does he have that I don't?"

Kax took a deep breath and looked Skyler in the eyes. "I think I love him and he is really sweet and kind. He is mature and stable in his career. Oh, and he loves being a pilot just like me. We can talk about ships and stars for hours."

Skyler took a step back, taking a seat on Perry's bed. "Okay, I can understand that. I know you have said you like mature guys, but he is in his 60s."

Kax looked up at Skyler. Her eyes were red and starting to water. "Please don't report me. Skyler, if you love me, please don't. We don't choose who we love."

Skyler took a deep breath and stared into Kax's teary eyes. "You're right. We don't get to choose who we love. I love you and I want to see you become a pilot. Heck, I want to see you become the best pilot, and as much as this is tearing me up inside I won't report you. But you better hope he loves you back. Because Kax, if he ever hurts you I will hurt him like he has hurt me okay?"

Tears ran down her face and she tried to smile. "Thank you, Skyler."

He got off the bed and walked over to the other bed and put his arm around her. He used his sleeve and wiped her tears away. "Come on, let's go get lunch."

She sniffled. Her nose was all puffy and her cheeks were red. She looked at her watch. "I don't think there is much time left."

Skyler reached into his drawer and pulled out a couple of tissues. He gave them to her, "Then we will just skip our next class." He looked at the time on her watch. "Actually let's skip the rest of the day and go to the city and have lunch there. Do you know the only time I have had the chance to go out and see the city was the first night when I got into town?"

She blew her nose. "But what about your extra credit work? Don't you have to be back at that?"

"Nah, Perry will cover for me. Right now, all that matters to me is making you happy."

"I have a car here. I will take you for a tour around the city." She wiggled her cat ears.

Chapter 7

Perry came back to the room later than usual with their new schedule. He saw Skyler lying on his bed playing with his tablet and shopping bags all over the floor. "So, there you are. You didn't come back from lunch. You went shopping? What happened to your perfect attendance?"

"Kax needed me and I felt that was more important." Skyler sat up, putting his tablet aside. "I bought you a few things. Your stuff is on your bed."

Perry walked over to his bed and looked in the bag. He pulled out the items one by one. There was a tabby cat plushie, a green t-shirt that said, 'I love plants' and a miniature seedling kit to grow about six plants. He looked back at Skyler. "This is awesome, thank you. But why the cat plushie?"

Skyler resisted the urge to laugh. "I got you a pussy. Now you can't say I'm inconsiderate and take all the girls."

Perry laughed and put the cat on the nightstand. "Cute. I'll treasure it always." He folded his shirt and placed it in his drawer. "So how did you get off base? You don't have a vehicle."

"Kax. She has a car here and we went out for lunch and then she showed me around town and we went shopping."

Perry looked at all of Skyler's bags. "I assume those are all clothes. Do you really need that many? We mostly wear our uniforms."

Skyler picked up one of the bags and put it on the bed. "They're not all clothes, but most of them. I'm going to be here for the next year at least so why not?"

Perry placed his mini greenhouse on the nightstand. "So you going to tell Kandice about your date with Kax?"

Skyler scoffed, taking the clothes out of their bags. "It wasn't a date. We just hung out as friends, nothing else. I don't see a reason to tell her. She doesn't tell me what she does daily. If she asks I will but I'm not going to call her up and say guess what, I went out shopping with my friend who happens to be a girl."

Perry unzipped his uniform, taking off his cadet jacket. "Makes sense. So why did you and Kax decide to go out for lunch?"

Skyler folded his shirts one by one and placed them in his drawer. He took a deep breath, "I found out who Kax is dating and it's a secret that she doesn't want out. If I tell you, you must promise not to report her. Michael is okay I plan to talk to him about this later."

Lowering his brow, Perry said, "I'm confused, what is going on? Who is she dating?"

Skyler looked down at his feet turning away from Perry. "Commodore Kreeve, her flight instructor."

His eyes widened. "You got to be kidding me, a commodore? He's got to be old. Why would she want to date an old guy like him? She is young and hot."

Skyler went back to putting his clothes away. "Exactly. Plus it is illegal, but she says she's in love with him and that he is more mature than me." He pulled out a bottle of grey hair dye out of the bag and put it on his desk.

Perry looked at the bottle of dye. "Um why do you have a bottle of grey hair color?"

Skyler smirked. "Not my best idea, but if Kax likes guys with grey hair I want to see if dying my hair grey will change her mind."

Laughing, Perry grabbed the bottle of dye off Skyler's desk. "You don't need dye. That's not going to help get her attention." He looked at the ingredients. "But we can use this for the research. There are a few chemicals in here that we need for the plants."

Skyler grabbed the bottle back. "It's my hair. I'm going to color it."

Perry got off his bed and took back the bottle of dye. "Skyler you're a blond. You don't want to color your hair, it looks great already. If you go grey and she doesn't like it what are you going to do? You will look too old to pick up chicks. Don't color it. Plus, you're a blond, you will go white not grey when you get older."

Skyler sighed. "I just want to know what makes me mature in her eyes? Is it my age or is it my attitude?"

Perry put his hand on Skyler's shoulder. "Just be there for her. One day she will realize that the guys she dates aren't as good as you and will come crawling."

Skyler shook his head. "I guess you're right." Skyler went back to unpacking his bags. He handed Perry a small cardboard box. "I forgot to put these in your bags. I used all yours up the other day."

Perry looked at the box in his hand. "A 50 pack of condoms. I don't think I have ever used that many."

Skyler pulled out own his box. "It was cheaper, and don't worry when I finish mine I will borrow yours again."

Perry looked nervous. "Just make sure you leave me at least one."

Skyler laughed, putting his box in the drawer. He opened the box and took five off the row and put them on top of the desk.

Perry looked at the ones on the top of the desk. "Why did you do that?"

Skyler grinned. "When a girl comes over don't show the girl you got fifty you show a couple so it looks like you're prepared. Fifty makes it look like you're sleeping with everyone."

Perry frowned. "But aren't you sleeping with everyone?"

Skyler laughed. "Not here. I haven't had time. As much as me and Kandy are casual I have been pretty steady with her."

There was a knock on their door. Skyler closed the drawer. "Come in!"

Kandice opened the door. "Hey Skyler. I was stopping by and wanted to know if you were interested?"

Skyler held up the condoms on the desk. "Oh, I'm interested."

She sighed. "Do we always have to use condoms?"

Skyler's chest tightened and he remembered Dr. Fogg's warning. "Unless you're on the pill or something, I'm not taking any chances. I don't want kids."

She pulled out a note out of her pocket and handed it to Skyler.

He looked at it. "This is a doctor's note saying you got an NBI, what's is that?"

Perry spoke up. "An NBI is a device that is inserted into a woman to stop her from reproducing until she has it removed and wants to have children."

Skyler wiped the sweat off his brow. "Oh good. I was almost worried you were trying to have my baby."

She sat on Skyler's bed. "You're my boy toy, why would I want a kid with you?"

Skyler chuckled. "Well I was warned by a few locals that a lot of the women here find boy toys, get pregnant for their genetics and then marry some other guy."

She burst out laughing. "No, it's not like that. Those women usually have partners who have problems having kids. Or must have a child to continue a bloodline but are in love with another. I'm not like that. I don't want kids, I want to have fun. I got a brother and sister who can have kids, and I would definitely not do that with an off worlder."

"What do you mean off worlder?"

She got up and kissed Skyler. "I like you but if I was going to get pregnant and marry another Catillion and if the father of my child is human the baby may have human ears and eyes and then how do I explain that?"

Skyler laughed and kissed her back. "Well if you're not going to make me a father, I'm happy to do whatever you want."

She played with his ear a bit. "No you won't be my baby daddy but I will be needing you to meet my daddy."

Skyler pushed her back. "No way. I've done that before. I'm not meeting another girl's parents."

She laughed. "It's not like that. My dad has come out here from Earth to see his kids and he wants us all to bring our partners. You're the closest I got so come to dinner this weekend."

Skyler took a deep breath. "Okay but just to let you know the last time I met a girl's parent's she tried to trap me into marriage."

Kandice laughed. "I have had five marriage proposals. I'm not saying yes to anyone yet. My family is used to me bringing home random guys."

"Will your mother be there?"

She shook her head. "No, my mother died when I was eight. She was a pilot in the war."

Perry held up his hand. "Um let me get this straight, you have a brother and sister, your mom's dead, your sister is a pilot and you were half raised on earth. By any chance-"

Skyler coughed. "Perry, this is not the time. Me and Kandy are about to go out."

"But Skyler doesn't her story sound like-"

Skyler kissed Kandy. "Perry there is no time. We will talk about it later." He took her hand and left the room.

Perry watched them leave. He sat down on the bed wondering if Kandice was by chance Kax's sister.

Skyler followed Kandice to the garage and got into the car with her. "So where are we going today?"

"Well, before we have sex I thought we could do some shopping." Kandice said.

Skyler laughed. "I just did some shopping earlier today. How about we just go out for dinner and dancing?"

"Sure, we could do that. I know a great bar we could get dinner at."

Skyler grinned, "You sure know what I like."

They soon got to the bar and grabbed a table. The bar was called The Red Dot and it was like many other buildings, cylinder structure with a round door. Inside it looked like your normal 20th century Earth sports bar.

"It's a sports bar? Why would you take me to a sports bar?" Skyler asked. "It is also a very old fashioned sports bar."

"Really, it took you 'til we got here to figure out it was a sports bar? Relax, they have great food, music and in the back there is a tattoo parlour." She picked a table in the middle of the room. "Also, this is a very modern design style for Catillion, but compared to Earth it looks outdated."

"We're not getting tattoos are we?" Skyler asked.

"Not unless you want one. I was merely just mentioning it. I was thinking of getting one but I'm still undecided. I have been thinking of getting a few little hearts down by my hip but I am not sure."

"That would look very sexy." Skyler said while picking up a menu. "Wow, these prices are cheap. I like it here."

Kandice looked at her own menu, "no they aren't, remember they are all in Catillion dollars. Have you had a chance to go to the currency exchange yet?"

"Right, 5 Catillion dollars is a lot of money." Skyler tossed his head back, "damn that is what I forgot to do sorry, is there an ATM nearby? I only have my cards."

"They don't take cards here. Don't worry about it, it's on me. You can pay me back in other ways." She placed her hand on Skyler's knee.

He grinned, "sounds good to me."

A waitress soon came over to take their order. Into the night when they had finished their food and had a handful for drinks Skyler blurted out. "you should get a tattoo. It would look sexy on you."

Kandice laughed, "Really you think so? What should I get it of?"

"Well you brought me here for some reason you could have picked any bar in the city but you choose this one. I think you secretly want one, and as for design, get what you told me about the little stars or hearts on your hips that would be so cute." Skyler suggested.

"I don't know. What about you? Is there anything you want to get done?"

Skyler took a sip of his beer, "Naw, tattoo's aren't for me."

"Not even a sailor's tattoo or something captain-like?" She finished off her beer.

"When I'm a captain, sure, I will consider it. Until then I'm good."

"What about an earring? They do piercings too. You would look really cute with one and they are traditional for sailors." She stretched her arm out and played with his ear.

He smiled at how playful she was being. "You really think it would look good on me?"

"I really do." She gave him a wink.

"How about this? We go back there and if you get this tattoo you want I get my ear pierced?" He flirted back.

"That sounds like a fun idea. It will make you look so sexy and mature." She played with her hair, flirting back.

"Speaking of mature, I bought a bottle of grey hair dye to make me look really mature." He smugly smiled.

"Yuck, grey hair is icky. Don't dye your hair. Actually you are a really nice blonde so don't ever ruin your hair by dyeing it. Find a better use for that dye." She got up out of her chair, "come on, time to go crazy."

Chapter 8

Skyler with a hangover rubbed his eyes as he got up to the alarm sound buzzing. He rubbed his neck and stretched.

Perry stared at Skyler. "Did you get your ear pierced?"

Skyler touched his sore left ear. "Oh ya, when I was out with Kandy last night she decided to get a tattoo and I got my ear pierced. Do you like it? She said it looked cute."

Perry examined the diamond in Skyler's ear. "You will literally do anything a girl says won't you?"

Skyler stepped back. "What is that supposed to mean?"

Perry raised an eyebrow at Skyler. "Really, you don't know? Come on, I have known you for a couple of years now and every time a woman tells you to do something, you do it. You're a sucker for women and you wrap yourself around their fingers. You're a victim of love."

"Prove it, Perry. I think you're just jealous I'm with a really hot babe and you can't get one," Skyler said.

"That earring is a great example. You did that because you wanted to or because Kandy told you to?" Perry paused for the moment, looking Skyler up and down and noticed the bottle of grey hair dye in his hand. "You brought that bottle of hair dye with you?"

Skyler raised his hand to argue back but paused. "I brought it here because you said it could be useful, and it turns out I didn't need it." He mumbled at the end.

"Uh huh. I count that as my point proven." Perry took the bottle of hair dye from Skyler. "Come on let's go give this to Dr. Fogg."

Dr. Fogg was jotting some things down in a notebook. He looked up at the boys. "Glad you two are finally getting to work. Skyler, did you get lost having lunch yesterday, should I tell you to bring a lunch from now on?"

Skyler laughed. "Naw, I bumped into Kax and we went to the city to go get some lunch and then went shopping. We got caught up on the summer."

Dr. Fogg examined a nearby plant, looking at its leaves then writing something down, "That's nice. Make sure you call me next time if you're not coming back. Poor Perry had to cover for you. I will make accommodations for you if I know you're not coming."

Perry held out the bottle of grey hair dye. "It's fine. I don't mind covering for him because guess what, Skyler solved our problem." He handed Dr. Fogg the bottle of dye. "Look at the ingredients. Three of the chemicals you need are in this. You said you couldn't find a source of them for this planet. Well, they're in this."

Dr. Fogg looked at the bottle and then at Skyler. "What were you doing with a bottle of grey hair dye?"

Skyler turned his head away. "I bought the wrong color."

Perry shook his head. "He was trying to impress a girl who likes older mature men. I told him he was stupid."

Dr. Fogg laughed. "Don't dye your hair for a girl. You look good with your hair, same color as your father's. Nice earring by the way."

Skyler stared at him. "You knew my father?"

Dr. Fogg patted Skyler on the back. "Kid everyone knew your dad. He was very well known. If they didn't serve with him they heard of his reputation."

"I hope it was a good one," Perry cut in.

"Well that was a matter of opinion. Your father liked to do things his way. He got away with that because the rules weren't so tight back then. He got the job done phenomenally but he also stepped on a lot of toes." Dr. Fogg paused. "Thinking about this reminds me he owes me a plant."

"Well sorry to tell you he is dead." Skyler looked nervous, "But I'm helping you with your plants does that count?"

"I know he is dead," Dr. Fogg narrowed his eyes. "You brought me the hair dye so I will count that as a down payment."

"How can someone owe you a plant?" Michael cut in.

Dr. Fogg laughed. "Back before I was a botanist with the forces I was a smuggler. As a botanist, I got free travel. I had a great scam going. I would find botany-related jobs on planets and then have to bring my plants which I would smuggle items in. Security never touched my plants and when I got to my destination I would make the deal and get my paycheck and then go to my botany job. I got paid twice to do the things I loved." He sat down in the closest chair. "One day I was being sent to Earth for a job to replant the president's garden. I also was hired to smuggle in some centurion crystals. So I packed my lilies and put the crystals in closed flowers so by the time I got to Earth they would bloom and I would collect the crystals."

"So what happened?" Skyler asked. "One bloomed too early?"

Dr. Fogg shook his head. "No, that would be too easy. Your father was too smart for me. He got a report about the robbery of the crystals. I didn't steal them, by the way. Someone else did. He was only doing his job and searched my stuff. I told him not to touch my plants. He knocked one over and cut it open. He found the crystals and I was arrested. The plants were safe. Once they bloomed they got their crystals back and I got my plants back. But they were expensive lilies and he killed one!" Fogg snapped.

Skyler pulled out his wallet. "So do you want me to pay for the replacement of one?"

Dr. Fogg shook his head. "They're extinct now. This story was almost 30 years ago. You will have to work off the debt."

Michael frowned. "So how did you end up working for the Forces?"

Dr. Fogg turned his attention to Michael. "Simple enough. I was given a choice: be handed over to the centurion government, or work off my sentence with the forces. I chose to work it off. I still got another 40 years left, but hey, at least I get to work with plants. Any other questions, boys?"

Skyler raised his hand. "Ya um, does this mean you hate my father for ruining your career?"

Dr. Fogg shook his head with a smile. "I may not be making anywhere near the amount of money I used to but I don't hate him. He did me a favor. This job gives me all the funding for plants I need, which is what I spent most of my smuggling money on anyway. Actually I like working with you, Skyler. It makes me feel like I'm paying your father back for helping me get on the right track."

Skyler was trying to absorb all this information. "So I owe you for a plant that doesn't exist anymore but you don't want money?"

"That's right, so get to work!"

Michael walked over to the potted plants and said, "can we get back to work? We need these leaves clipped before there are more dead ones and before we start the next step."

Perry rushed over to the plants and grabbed a set of clippers. "Oh boy, this is going to be fun!"

Dr. Fogg walked off towards his lab on the other side of the room. "I have to separate these chemicals then I will be back. Keep on clipping, Michael knows everything we need to do." He walked away and locked himself in his office.

Skyler grabbed a set of clippers and walked over to the plants. He knelt down next to Michael. His chest was heavy but he knew he needed to ask. "Michael, did you know Kax has a boyfriend?"

Michael rolled his eyes. "Yes, she told me and do not dare think about trying to break them up. Let her be happy for once."

Skyler clipped off a few dead leaves. "I do want to break them up but not for personal gain. I'm just curious, Michael do you know who Kax is dating?"

Michael shook his head focusing on the plants. "As long as it's not me or you I do not care."

Perry poked his head up. "He already told me and you will want to know who it is."

Michael shook his head. "Fine then tell me. Who is it?"

Skyler took a deep breath. "She is dating Commodore Kreeve, her flight instructor."

Michael's eyes widened and he dropped his clippers. "What? Does she know that is illegal?"

Skyler nodded. "She knows. I talked to her about it yesterday. She says she loves him."

Michael frowned. "How did you find out about this? Surely she would not tell you willingly?"

Skyler kept clipping the trees. "I went to take her for lunch and I saw her giving him a blowjob in the classroom. I waited until she was done and then talked to her. You have to promise not to report her. I want them broken up, then we can ruin his career and not hers."

Perry laughed. "That's how you found out? Talk about hard evidence. Wow!"

Skyler closed his eyes and let out a little laugh. "Yup that's how I found out. You're making it sound better than it was."

"Skyler," said Michael, "this is really making me feel uncomfortable now. It's one thing for them to be seeing each other on their own time, but during school hours? That's not right at all. I thought you were the stupid one." Michael got up off the floor and stormed his way to the door.

Skyler dropped his clippers and got up. "Perry, cover for us." He ran out the door after Michael.

He chased Michael down the hall. *Damn I wish I had long legs like Michael it would make this a lot easier.* They left the building and soon Skyler realized where Michael was heading. He bolted with all his strength to catch Michael. He saw Michael about to open the door to building C. Skyler took a leap at Michael, knocking him to the ground.

Michael glared back at Skyler. "Let me go, Skyler!"

Skyler gripped Michael's waist tight not letting go. "I let you go and what do you think you will do? If you expose Kax in class you will ruin both their careers, let alone have her hate you for the rest of her life. I know it is wrong but damn it we can't do anything about it yet!"

Michael took a deep breath. He was silent for a moment. "Fine I will not do anything. Could you please let me up?"

Skyler let go of Michael's waist, stood up and dusted himself off. "I don't like this any more than you do. But there is nothing we can do. Kax has to make her own mistakes. You always let me make mine."

Michael picked himself off the ground. He dusted himself off and glared at Skyler. "I know you are not stupid but you are naive so I think you need to make a few of your own mistakes. I always thought Kax was better than this. What reason did she give? Why would she date him?"

"He was older and mature. Remember how she is always telling me she wants someone who is mature? Ya, she means grey hair and wrinkles."

Michael let out a little laugh. "Really? I thought she just wanted you to stop drinking. You are at least 20 years away from white hair."

Skyler sighed. "That's why I bought the bottle of dye."

Michael shook his head. "So what do we do about this?"

Skyler shrugged. "No idea, wait for him to slip up and beat the crap out of him? That's what I'm waiting for."

Michael looked down at his feet. "That might be our only option. I just hope he doesn't hurt her or mess up her career."

Skyler's eyes flared. "If he harms her career in any way I will make him pay for it, even if I have to give up mine."

Michael raised an eyebrow at Skyler. "No one will be giving up or ruining their career over this. Except commodore Kreeve. He is the one who is guilty."

Skyler smiled and patted Michael on the back. "Come on let's get back to the plants."

Dr. Fogg greeted them when they got back to the lab. "It's nice that you are getting out more Michael but please give me a warning next time you are going to run out of here with Skyler."

Michael put his head down. "I am sorry, sir. It will not happen again."

Dr. Fogg shook his head. "No need to apologize. Perry explained it to me."

Skyler snarled at Perry. "What did you tell him? I told you not to tell anyone!"

Dr. Fogg held Skyler back. "I will not report this. But I'm adding it onto your debt. This is serious, but who am I to judge? Just don't let this interfere with your work anymore."

Skyler and Michael nodded their heads. Michael went back to work.

"I'm going to recommend you start going to the Cat Scratch bar from now on." Dr. Fogg pulled Skyler aside and whispered. "Now get back to work! No more interruptions!"

Chapter 9

Lying in bed next to Kandice, Skyler kissed her on the lips. He placed his hand on her face and smiled.

"Do you really have to go to class this early?" She asked playing with his ear.

He gazed into her eyes. "I'm sorry. I wish I could spend more time with you. Don't worry I will see you tonight then we can go for dinner."

She twirled her finger in one of his curls. "Is this what it is like being a captain's girl?"

Skyler shrugged. "I don't know. I haven't had one yet. I think you would see me more because you could come onto the bridge and sit on my lap, if you know what I mean." He winked.

She playfully pushed him back. She then leaned in and kissed him one more time on the lips. "You will like my family. You have nothing to worry about."

Skyler's hand shook. "I don't doubt you have a nice family. I just don't like meeting parents."

She laughed one more time, then got out of the bed and proceeded to get dressed.

He watched her put on her clothes, slipping on her pants one leg at a time, slowly putting her bra on and then rolling down her t-shirt. "I'm not sure what is sexier, me taking them off you or you putting them back on."

She turned around and rubbed his leg. "You can take them off tonight. Until then, don't get too excited."

He sat up and leaned over trying to kiss her.

She moved away, "No more fun 'til tonight."

He pouted his face. "Oh come on, just a little bit more to get me through the day."

She slipped on her shoes and smiled. "You can wait. Waiting is half the fun." She pulled him close to her lips going to kiss him. Then pushed him away. "See you tonight." She got up off the bed, shaking her tails as she walked out of the room.

Perry came in a moment later in his uniform, carrying a small plastic take out container. "Here's your breakfast since you decided to stay in bed."

Skyler sat up and took the container out of his hands. "Thanks buddy, you know I'm not really a morning person."

Perry looked down and picked up a red lace thong off the floor. "I'm guessing you already ate?" He dropped the thong on Skyler's bed.

Skyler laughed, opening the container and looking inside. "Fruit? You brought me fruit? What happened to toast or bacon?"

Perry handed Skyler a fork. "That's all that was left, the cats took all the meat products. You want better food next time you go down there. Kax missed you."

Skyler looked up at Perry. "You had breakfast with Kax? I thought her flight training got her up before dawn on Fridays?"

Perry went over to check on his plants. "It does, for her this was lunchtime. But it's fine she understands. She is used to not seeing you at breakfast time."

Skyler ate a few pieces of fruit. "Breakfast is not my favorite meal of the day. Sorry."

Perry sat on his bed. "So do you want to go to the bar tonight?"

Skyler finished his fruit. "I would love to but I got to meet Kandice's family tonight. I'm not looking forward to it." He put the container on the desk and got up out of bed to get dressed.

Perry laughed. "Dude, you will be fine and I guess I will go drinking with Michael tonight."

Skyler put on his pants. "If you can convince him. But hey, you should go to the Cat Scratch bar. I haven't been there yet but I have been recommended to go there."

Perry pulled out his tablet. "I don't know if I can get there, you need a car if it's off campus."

Skyler finished putting on his black undershirt and grabbed the tablet. "It's not that far, if you want, I can convince Kandice to give you a lift."

Perry frowned taking his tablet back. "Then how am I supposed to get back?"

Skyler reached over to his desk and grabbed his wallet. He pulled out some money. "Here's a 100 that should be enough take a cab, or convince a hot girl to drive you home."

Perry took the money. "Why are you insisting I go to this bar? Why can't I just go to the campus one? More human chicks there."

Skyler frowned. "Do it Perry, I want to know why I was told to go there. I would be going myself but I'm tied up tonight, and I thought you liked these cat girls."

Perry shrugged. "I guess if you insist I will go. And I do like these cats but there are so many of them here. I want something more exotic."

Skyler put on his cadet jacket and patted Perry on the back. "There should be something exotic there. This planet isn't all monotone. Come on, it's time to get to class."

Perry got up. "Aye Captain!"

＊

Skyler put on his new dark blue jeans and a tight dark green t-shirt. He brushed his hair in the mirror.

Perry entered the room. He looked at Skyler and laughed, "dude did you try on those pants before you bought them?"

Skyler turned around looked at his pants. "No what do you mean?"

Perry reached behind Skyler and poked his butt. "They have a tail hole in them. They're made for cats."

Skyler turned his hips to the mirror and saw the hole. "Damn it. Why would I think to look for tail holes?" He quickly took his pants off. "Let's see if the other pairs have them. Not all cats have tails." He pulled all his new pants out of the drawers.

Perry laughed. "You know you could just wear them backwards and save time."

Skyler threw a pair at Perry. "You could just wear them and save the guys some time."

Perry grumbled. "If you want I will sew the holes up for you. They do look good on you."

Skyler shook his head. "Only three of the pairs have tail holes. I still have the tags on them. I will just exchange them."

Perry picked up another pair. "See, here on the tag it says size 32T I think that means tail. Because this one doesn't have the T on them. Surprised Kax didn't tell you about that."

Skyler quickly put on the new pair of pants. "I guess it slipped her mind." He placed the non-tail ones back in his drawer. He looked back at Perry. "You going to get dressed for the bar?"

Perry grabbed one of Skyler's pairs of pants out of the drawer. "Just for the gay comment, I'm stealing one of your pairs of pants."

Skyler glared. "Keep them. You just owe me $50 for them."

Perry's eyes widened. "You spent $50 dollars a pair? And you bought how many?"

Skyler fixed his hair one more time. "Seven, but I spent more than that. You saw the bags. I bought a whole new wardrobe for me and Kax."

Perry put on the pants. "You need to take me shopping sometime. I bet you spend more money on Kax than her boyfriend does."

Skyler cringed at the mention of Commodore Kreeve. "I bought her a car and a house, remember. I would like to see any guy spend more on her."

Kandice stepped into the room. "Hey Skyler, are you ready?"

Skyler turned around and smiled. "Ya, I'm ready. We just need to wait for Perry to get dressed."

She looked confused. "Why do we have to wait for Perry?"

He put his hand on her hips and pulled her closer. "We're giving him a ride to the Cat Scratch bar."

Kandice gave a disgusted look. "He's too young. That bar is for girls who want old guys and guys who want to pick up young girls. Unless it is ladies' night and he wants to pick up a granny, he will have no luck at all."

Skyler frowned. "Really? I was recommended to go there. I was going to get Perry to check it out for me. But now that you tell me that… Perry, just go to the campus bar."

Perry put on a tight black t-shirt. "Yeah, any women over 40 I'm really not interested in but I wouldn't object."

Kandice shot him an odd look. "You would sleep with a 40 year old and you're how old?"

Perry put on Skyler's leather jacket. "21 and I mean that not as a one night stand I mean to date. That's my limit. You never know unless you keep your options open."

Skyler walked over and grabbed a condom out of Perry's drawer and handed it to him. "Go bang a young cadet today. You need it."

Perry took the condom and put it in his pocket. "I will do my best. I'm borrowing your girl-getting jacket, and going to start walking to the campus bar." Perry headed towards the door.

Skyler smiled. "Don't lose that jacket or you're paying me back for it."

Perry waved goodbye and he left the room.

Kandice kissed Skyler. "You should pack some condoms for tonight."

He looked confused. "Why do I need to pack condoms? You still have your implant in, right?"

She nodded. "I do but I have been telling my sister about you and how great you are. So there's a chance you might get with her."

Skyler blushed. "What have you been telling her? Are we giving her a ride?"

She played her fingers up and down his chest. "All the good things, like your magic tongue and your other talents. She will meet us there. She got off class earlier so she went home on her own."

Skyler smiled. "Does she have a boyfriend?"

Kandice bit her lips. "Well, yes she does. But I doubt he will be there tonight. I really don't think he is that good of a guy. I don't think it will last with him. She isn't too happy."

Skyler put on his jacket. "Well then, I can't wait to meet your sister."

She pulled out her set of keys. "Well then let's get going."

They pulled up to the driveway of her dad's place. He saw two other cars in the driveway. One a van and the other a blue sedan.

Skyler looked up at the house. It was a small blue box built on a hill with a round door. "That's a small house. How many of you lived in there?"

Kandice laughed. "It's bigger than it looks. There is an upstairs. But this is my grandparents' house. So only me, Tom and his girlfriend live here. On Earth my dad owns a condo and he recently sold the big house. Tom mostly lives here now because it is closer to his doctors. When we were kids he went for treatment on Earth. I live here now because I'm in college, my sister stayed on Earth to go to the academy, my Dad lives on Earth and visits us often."

"Are your grandparents going to be here?"

She shook her head, parking the car. "No they died a couple of years ago. They left me the house."

Skyler widened his eyes. "You have your own house and we have to keep breaking the rules and staying in my room? Why didn't you tell me? We could have spent weekends here and you drive me to work."

She laughed, taking her seat belt off. "We're not that serious. You're not living with me. Plus, you would have to put up with Tom."

Skyler took his seat belt off. "I thought you said I would like Tom?"

She leaned over and kissed him. "Let's just go in, sweetie, and make any big decisions after."

He got out of the car and followed Kandice to the door.

She grabbed his hand as she opened the door. "Hi everyone, look who I brought!"

Skyler's eyes widened and he squeezed Kandice's hand when he saw the tall older blonde Catillion glaring at him.

He tried to bolt for the door, but she was holding him back.

The man got up off the couch and went right up to Skyler. "Skyler Therris! You're the one who's sleeping with my daughter?"

Kandice looked at Skyler. "You know my dad?"

Skyler let go of her hand, and backed up against the wall. "Uh ya, I met David last year. My uncle bought your family's cabin from him. Kandice, remember that girl I told you I liked but she has a boyfriend? I guess that's your sister Kax. She has been my friend since I joined the academy."

Kandice covered her face and laughed. "Oh my, I had no idea. I guess we need to talk more."

David grabbed Skyler's shoulder and pulled him over to the couch. "She's right, we do need to talk more." He pushed Skyler down onto the couch.

Kax walked into the room and saw Skyler on the couch. "Skyler, what are you doing here?"

Skyler waved to her awkwardly. "Hey Kax, turns out I have been dating your sister."

Kax rolled her eyes. "Oh Skyler, I should have guessed it was you."

David sat on the coffee table in front of Skyler. "What are your intentions with my daughter?"

With his eyes bulging, sweat running down his face he swallowed. "Well sir, I love Kax and I mean her no harm. If I knew Kandice was her sister, I would have never touched her. Kax is a lovely girl and the love of my life, I'm willing to do anything for her to make her happy."

David stared into his eyes. "I wasn't talking about Kax, I was talking about Kandice. She is the one you're dating."

Skyler looked at Kandice then back at David. "Well she is a lovely woman and I'm honored to be her boyfriend but my future with her is entirely in her hands."

David lifted his hand up to speak again when a young blonde Catillion wheeled into the living room followed by a calico hair colored lady. "Dad, don't harass another one of Kax's boyfriends. You do want grandkids?"

David turned his head. "He's Kandice's boyfriend, but has an interest in your other sister. And I don't want grandkids from Captain Therris's son."

Tom's ears picked up. "That's Skyler? He's not at all what I expected. I thought he would have taken after his mother more."

Skyler turned to Tom and frowned. "How do you know my mother?"

Tom smiled. "The newspaper. My mom kept a scrapbook of your father and the funeral. Once my dad met your dad and didn't stop ranting about him for a week. I also asked Kax about you. But you really do look like a younger version of your father. No wonder my dad is so mad."

David hissed at Tom. "Shut up Tom. No speaking about him and her in this house."

Tom glared. "Did you even make an effort to learn about Mom's work? Did you ever once pick up one of her flight books and at least make the effort to try and learn something about what she did? She loved you and was not going to leave you. She told me all about this as a child. Skyler is no threat to you."

Kax went over and sat next to Skyler on the couch. "Dad, Skyler is just a friend who has a crush on me. If I choose to be with him in the future, then that is my choice but right now he is dating Kandice but still is my friend."

David glared at his daughter. "There was a time when your mother told me that Levi was just her captain but she was lying about that."

"Sir, I mean your daughters no harm. I love Kax and I like Kandice. If you give me a chance I will prove to you I'm not a bad guy. I can't control what my father did but I know he wouldn't have done it without a good reason." Skyler was shaking, thinking, *Please don't kill me.*

David stood up and punched Skyler in the stomach. "You hurt my daughters or make them cry I will kill you." He got up and made his way towards the kitchen.

Skyler curled in pain.

Kandice went to his side and rubbed his back. She gave him a kiss on the cheek. "Oh sweetie, you're going to be okay. I'm sorry he hurt you."

A woman's voice called from the kitchen. "Dinner is ready! You all better get in here before it gets cold!"

They all started making their way to the kitchen

Skyler got up slowly, grabbing his stomach.

Kax went to his side helping him stand up straight. She whispered into his ear. "I'm sorry about my father. If I had known you were my sister's boyfriend I would have told you not to come."

Skyler glared at Kax. "Is that what you told your boyfriend? I wish he was here. It would take the heat off me."

Kax took a deep breath. "I will do my best to help you, but after tonight you are going to dump my sister."

Skyler shook his head. "Not until you break up with your boyfriend."

Kax frowned as they made their way to the kitchen. Skyler sat down at the rectangular table at the opposite end of David. Kax and Kandice on the side and David and his girlfriend on the other. He looked around the teal kitchen. It was small with a bay window at the far side, with white countertops and pale wood cupboards.

The lady next to Tom brought the food over to the table and began to serve everybody.

Tom turned to Skyler. "Skyler, this is my fiancé Layla. She made dinner."

Skyler smiled and Layla handed him a plate of food. "It's nice to meet you and the food smells great."

She smiled back. "It's nice to meet you too."

Skyler looked back at Tom. "It is nice to meet you both. I must say you all make a lovely family. Tom you and Layla make a lovely couple."

Layla blushed and sat back down. "Why thank you, Skyler. Me and Tom have been together for two years now, and last month he popped the question."

"Well congratulations, I'm happy for you." He looked down at his plate. There was a steak, raw carrots and a foreign hard pellet like grain. He picked up a spoonful and held it up. "Um what is this?"

Kax laughed. "You don't have to eat that, Skyler, it might break your teeth. It's called schmillet. It's a grain that's soft when picked then you roast it and it is really good."

"I'm sorry, Skyler, if I would have known Kandice was bringing a human for dinner I would have made something else." Layla went to get up. "I'll make you something else."

It wasn't the only thing on the menu but he certainly didn't want her to make him something else. He was the guest. "No, please sit down. I'm fine, really."

Layla sat back down. "Well just don't go telling people I'm a bad cook."

Skyler took a bite of his steak and shook his head. "That's the exact opposite of what I will tell people."

David glared at Skyler from across the table. "Before I left Earth I saw in the paper there was a new member added to your family. How does it feel to be a big brother?"

Skyler shot a glare back. "I have no idea. I was only there for the birth. Haven't spoken to them since."

David played with his food. "So your mother remarried. I can't say I blame her. I mean after what your father did to her."

"What's that supposed to mean? You never remarried. By the way, my mother was the one who broke my dad's heart." Skyler made a fist. "David, I thought we got along last year. What's changed?"

Kax looked at her father. "Daddy, don't say things like that to Skyler."

"What's changed is you're now dating one of my daughters, and live with the other one on Earth!" David turned his glare to his daughter. "Why not, Kax? He knows our dirty little secret now we can know his. And by the way, I never remarried because I had three kids to raise."

Skyler took a deep breath, *There is only one way I'm going to get out of this.* He finished his bite of food. "My mother refused to take me to space and it broke my father's heart. She became cold and bitter. Near the end they were really just married on paper. Once my father was gone it took her no time to find another man. But it didn't work out and she got back with her high school lover Charles, who is the last person who should be a father or a politician. What else would you like to know? Would you like to know what it was like growing up with a mother who pushed you aside and never believed you when your step-father was beating you when she turned her back? I know you don't like my father, but if adultery was his only crime then he is still better than the set I have now. I'm sorry if my relationship with your daughters bothers you but I didn't know they were sisters."

The room was silent. All eyes were on Skyler and David, waiting for David to make the next move. He took a few more bites of his food. He looked right at Skyler for a moment. He got up out of his chair. "Thank you, Layla, for the lovely meal, but I must retire. I will see you in the morning. I have a lot of think about." He pushed his chair in and walked away.

All eyes were on Skyler.

Oh shit what did I do? He looked around with terror in his eyes.

Kax got up out of her chair and ran after her father.

Skyler's heart raced. "Did I say something wrong?"

Tom spoke up. "No, you said the truth. Kax and Dad are just close is all. Anything to do with Mom still bothers him."

"He was the one being an ass. You have done nothing wrong." Kandice said, going back to her food.

"I didn't mean to speak out of line. I didn't mean to ruin dinner."

Tom laughed. "You didn't, and trust me if Kax's boyfriend would have shown up it would have been a lot worse."

Skyler's eyes widened. "You know about Commodore Kreeve too, and you're okay with it?"

Tom shook his head. "My sister has bad taste in men. She hasn't brought home anyone in a while but we always knew she would end up dating her flight instructor."

Kandice laughed. "Ya she's like mom. Likes old men who are in control."

Skyler frowned. "How long have you two known about my dad and your mom?"

Tom and Kandice shared a look then he said, "I knew when I was a kid. Mom told me about it during my physio. Kandice found out when she was a teen when she found an old photo. But Dad kept Kax protected. He didn't want any of us to know."

Skyler nodded. "Ya, Cane told us. My mom never told me, but she never really talked about my father."

"You really don't have a nice mother do you?" Layla asked.

Skyler shook his head. "I used to like her, but the older I get, the more reasons I'm finding not to."

***

Skyler sat with Kandice on the couch in the living room watching the television. "Do we have to watch this silly movie? Can't we watch porn instead?"

Tom laughed. "No we can't just watch porn. Plus, this is a good movie. Enjoy it."

Kandice cuddled closer to Skyler putting her hand on his thigh. "Watch this movie and we can make our own porn after."

Skyler kissed her. "You know I love my piece of Kandy."

Kax came down the stairs. She looked like she had been crying. She sat down on the couch next to Skyler.

Skyler moved away from Kandice and looked at Kax. "Hey, are you all right?"

Kax nodded her head. "I'm fine, we just had an emotional conversation is all. You're allowed to date my sister, by the way. He is giving you a chance."

Skyler looked at Kax. "If you ever want to talk, you know I'm here for you."

She put on a soft smile. "I know you are, and thank you."

When the movie was done Tom let out a long yawn. "I think it is time to go to bed."

Kax rubbed her face. "Ya, I think so too." She got up off the couch.

Skyler smiled at Kax. "Sleep well."

Kax smirked back. "Don't be too loud tonight."

Skyler laughed. "I'm not the loud one."

Kax waved goodbye and went down the hall to her bedroom next to Tom's.

Kandice waved to her sister. "Good night. We're going to bed now as well." She got off the couch and took Skyler's hand. Helping him up, she kissed him on the lips. "Come sweetie, you're sleeping in my room tonight."

Skyler looked nervous. "Are you sure we should with your dad in the house?"

She walked Skyler up the stairs. "It's my house and you're my boy. I'm going to do what I want and who I want."

Skyler followed her up to her room and down the hall. He watched her open the door to reveal a large bedroom with a queen size bed, light blue walls, rose colored sheets with lots of pillows.

She stepped into the room and started taking off her clothes. He pointed to the door on the left and said, "there's a bathroom right there in case you need it."

Skyler watched her slip off her t-shirt revealing a blue lace bra. Slowly she took off her pants and revealed a matching blue lace thong. She let her clothes drop to the floor. She slipped into the bed.

He quickly took off his shirt and unzipped his pants and removed his underwear. He jumped into bed buck naked and immediately began kissing Kandice all the way from her lips to her thighs. He gently caressed her hips and slowly removed her panties. He kissed her inner thighs. Her purrs guided his moves.

She purred louder and louder as he stayed between her legs. She held his head down, just when she thought she could not take anymore.

He picked up his head and made his way back up. He kissed her neck and then her lips. He unhooked her bra and rubbed his face in her breasts. He sucked her nipples and positioned his hips and prepared to enter.

She let out a little, 'meow.'

He smiled and thrusted in and out. He kissed her lips and thrusted quickly in and out.

Her purring got louder and louder until she let out a loud meow.

He rolled over onto his back, panting heavily.

She rolled onto her side, running her fingers up and down her chest. "You were amazing."

He grinned, kissing her on the forehead. "No you're amazing," he said before rolling over and falling asleep.

Dawn came and a beam of light shone through the window right into Skyler's eyes. He grabbed the blanket and covered both himself and Kandice in the blanket.

She woke up and turned around to look at him. "What are you doing?"

He made sure no light could get in. "The suns up and it's in my eyes. I didn't want it to hurt your eyes too."

She leaned over and kissed him. "Catillions can adjust to the bright lights quicker, but thank you, sweetie, for being so kind." She poked her head out of the blankets, being careful not to let the light get in Skyler's eyes. She looked at the clock. "It's 5 a.m. We got to get going."

"What are you talking about? I don't start work until eight today." His voice was muffled by the covers.

She closed her blinds to block out some of the light. "Is that better?" She started getting dressed. "I know, but my dad's going to get up and I don't know how he will act today."

Skyler sat up in the bed. "No problem, but can I have a quick shower first?"

She walked over seductively. "Do you want me to join you?"

"You bet I do." He grinned as she got out of bed. He made his way to the shower.

Chapter 10

Perry was making his way back to the room when he ran into Skyler in the hall. "What are you doing back so early?"

Skyler looked at Perry. "What are you doing walking around the halls this early?"

Perry looked down at the ground. "Let's get to the room and I will explain."

Skyler looked suspicious, but made his way into the room. He noticed their beds had not been slept in. He turned to Perry. "What did you do?"

Perry sat down on the bed. "Remember how I said I would be willing to sleep with an older woman?"

Skyler's eyes widened. "You didn't. What was it like?"

Perry stared towards the ceiling. "I went to the bar with Michael. He had two drinks then left. I stayed and there was this lovely woman who came by my table, and we had a few drinks. It thought she was about 35 but once my head cleared she was more like 50. And she is Commodore Stellik. She teaches engineering and she has seen me around and thought I was cute."

Skyler laughed. "Well, you're not her student so it is not illegal, but not recommended."

Perry stopped Skyler. "That's not the worst part. She wants to see me again."

Skyler rubbed his face. "You have got to be kidding me. You sure know how to pick women. What race is she by the way?"

Perry closed his eyes. "I believe she is a Squallite."

"I hope she didn't try and sit on you." Skyler rolled on his bed, not able to stop laughing.

Perry pulled out his tablet and did a search. "She's only 7'5" and she's not too bad looking in this photo."

Skyler got up and grabbed the tablet from Perry. "That's her? She's not too bad and she has a good record. They do live longer than humans, so maybe she is worth going out with again. As long as she's not too much to handle."

Michael walked into the room. "You guys ready to go?"

Skyler handed the tablet to Michael. "Look at Perry's new girlfriend!"

"She's a Squallite." Michael raised an eyebrow at Perry then looked at the tablet. "She's a bit old, don't you think?"

"She's not my girlfriend, she picked me up after you left the bar and wants to see me again," Perry said, taking back the tablet. "Why do we need to get ready? We have two hours before we need to show up today."

Michael took the tablet back and opened Perry's e-mails and pulled up the one from Dr. Fogg and handed it back. "There you go. He sent it last night. We need to be there earlier now. If you two weren't out all night you would know this."

Perry read the e-mail and rubbed his head. "I don't think we can call in sick today, can we?"

Michael shook his head. "Today is important, we need to finish up some tests and get ready to harvest. And once they are harvested, we need to test them."

Skyler started getting dressed. He looked at Michael while he zipped up his cadet jacket, "Michael, all you think about is work. What is the big deal about these plants?"

Michael's eyes bulged. "Really? You do not know what the importance of renewable weapons that can be grown on ships and be used as a ration source means? Skyler, if this works, the future of weaponry is changed forever. I will get actual credit for it. You know what they did to me with the Jonesium. Sure they named it after me, gave me a cheque, but they put my name in tiny print so no one realizes who I am. Yet they are still using my invention on the new ships."

Skyler finished putting his pants on. "And this time it will be different. Michael, you're a genius and these plants are important, but you are not going to get a ton of credit. All these inventions are doing is buying you time away from the front lines. So I hope for you when these plants work you have another one up your sleeve."

Michael glared at Skyler. "You can be a real jerk sometimes." He turned around and left the room in a hurry.

Perry looked at Skyler. "Why would you say something to him like that?"

Skyler combed his hair in the mirror. "Because it is the truth, somebody had to say it."

Perry frowned. "You didn't have to say it like that!"

Skyler tossed his comb on to the bed. "Perry, I know you love plants, but you know they are probably going to give you more credit for these pants than Michael. They are going to be looking for any excuse to not give a Squallite credit. Which is why I don't want to have any part of them. I want them to give as much credit as they can to Michael."

Perry fixed up his uniform. "Well maybe things will be different."

Skyler shook his head and went to the door. "I only wish they could be." He made his way to the door.

***

Dr. Fogg was in the greenhouse tagging the plants with green, yellow, orange and red tags.

Michael stormed in and kicked over one of the plants.

"Don't touch the plants!" Dr. Fogg's eyes flashed and rushed over to Michael. He picked up the plant. "Michael, what has gotten into you?"

Breathing really heavy, Michael dropped to the floor and sat in the fetal position. "I am not going to be getting credit for these plants, am I?"

Dr. Fogg knelt down next to Michael. He put his hand on his shoulder. "I don't know but I do know you are going to change the world with these plants and for the better."

Michael looked at him. "What good can come from something that kills somebody?"

"Well for one thing, they are lightweight use, renewable sources and their beans are a source of food. If you're in a survival situation they will help you. People will die, but less will die and get hurt from making guns, they don't do damage if you aim them like if you were to shoot a gun. They're almost as good as a Swiss army knife with protein pills. People will die, but it will save many lives and do less damage. You can't ask for a better weapon. I will do all in my power to make sure you get credit for this invention. You're a genius who has proven himself beyond what Commodore Grey sent me in your files. If I have it my way you will never see the frontlines and you will get as much credit as you deserve."

Michael turned his wet eyes to Dr. Fogg. He brushed his hair back to reveal his tipless ears. "But I am a Squallite."

Dr. Fogg smiled. "On Earth you are, here you are just another sentient being. Humans may not recognize your work but the Catillions will."

Michael wiped the tears off his face. "Thank you for your reassurance, sir."

Dr. Fogg shook his head. "Stop calling me sir or Dr. Fogg. Call me James, that's my first name."

Michael got up and smiled. "Whatever you say, James."

Chapter 11

Perry and Skyler got to the greenhouse. They entered the room. Perry saw Michael and Dr. Fogg tagging the plants. He called out. "We're here and ready to start work."

Dr. Fogg stood up and called back. "Find the plants with the green tags and start harvesting. There is a basket on the side you can put them in there. Once you're done, I'll give you your orders."

Skyler followed Perry to the green tagged plants. Perry gave Skyler a basket and picked up another. "You start at one end, I will start at the other."

Skyler took the basket and walked to the end. He grabbed one large L shaped bean pod and picked them one by one. He called out to Michael. "How sexually repressed are you to create a weapon that looks like a large green dildo?"

Michael hollered back: "if you shove it up your ass it will poison you. I do not think you want to try."

"Poisonous dildos? Just because you're not getting laid doesn't mean everyone else has to suffer." Perry called out, jokingly.

Dr. Fogg spoke up, "they do have a point. Plants' fruit usually does look phallic or vaginal. It's part of nature. But in this case, we tried our best to make it look more like a plant gun. This is our third attempt. Everything else seems to be right."

Skyler grabbed one and pretended to suck on one.

Perry watched and laughed.

"That better be working I'm hearing." Dr. Fogg called out.

"James, there seems to be a problem with one of the plants." Michael called out.

Dr. Fogg quickly got up and walked over to the plant.

Perry's eyes widened. *The Dr. James Fogg? No, it can't be.* He called over to Skyler. "Skyler, come here. I need your help."

Skyler got up and walked over. "What is it?"

Perry whispered quietly. "Did he just call him James?"

Skyler nodded. "That's what I heard."

Perry pulled Skyler closer to him. "He's not just an ex-smuggler, he's Dr. James Fogg. This man is a psychopath and not to be trusted. We got to get out of here."

Skyler shook his head. "Perry, the guy has been here for the last six years. I think he is okay. You heard him, he has changed his life. I don't think we have anything to worry about."

Perry whispered to Skyler, trying to make sure Dr. Fogg couldn't hear them. "This man killed colony H and almost killed other colonies. I can prove it. Tonight I will look it up and show you. I have no idea why the Forces are letting him live. He is dangerous."

Skyler got up. "I think we can trust him, at least for now." He went back to picking the bean guns.

Perry watched from between the plants as the man helped Michael.

"Skyler, Perry, come over here and see this. We might have discovered something new about these plants."

The boys got up and made their way over.

Dr. Fogg held in his hand what looked to be two of the bean guns but joined at the head.

Perry looked at it in curiosity. "We have 2000 plants, how did this one grow like that sir?"

Dr. Fogg replied, "this was one of the plants we grew under the gas radiation. It must have caused it to grow like this. This plant is off limits until I can study it further."

Michael looked at the plants around it. "James, all the plants with the gas radiation have grown conjoined pods."

Dr. Fogg pulled out a package of purple tags out of his pocket and marked all five of the gas radiation bean plants. "No one is to touch these until I say so." He then picked up one of the plants and carried it off to his office.

Perry waited until Dr. Fogg left the room. He then went over to Michael and said, "why were you calling Dr. Fogg James?"

Michael looked at him oddly. "Because James is his name."

Perry shook his head. "You're joking, right? You do know that Dr. James Fogg is the man who almost wiped out all the space colonies? He is much more than a simple smuggler."

Michael shrugged. "Well maybe it was another, or James could be his middle name. I do not know, but why would they let someone with such a large criminal offense join the forces?"

Perry shook his head. "I don't know. But if it is not him this seems really strange."

Skyler then whispered. "He's coming back. Let's get back to work and solve this mystery later."

They nodded and went back to their jobs.

***

Later that night, Skyler was changing out of his uniform and into his bar clothes.

Perry was looking around on his tablet. "Damn it, Skyler, I cannot find his name anywhere online. I know it was him!"

"Are you sure you remember his name right? Maybe you got the wrong guy." Skyler slid on a pair of blue jeans.

Perry shook his head. "I know it's him. I just don't know why the records have been wiped."

Skyler rubbed his face and grabbed Perry's tablet. He scrolled around looking for some kind of info. "Who was the one who told you these stories about him?"

Perry scratched his head. "It was my dad. He is the one who told me. He has lived on the colonies his whole life. He could point him out."

Skyler combed his hair and handed Perry the tablet back. "Well in that case, I would call your dad and ask him. Then get a photo of the guy and show him to make sure you got the right one."

Perry nodded. "That sounds like a good idea. I haven't called my parents in a while. They must be worried about me."

Skyler took his leather jacket out of the closet and put it on. "I'm going to hang out with Kax and Michael tonight. You sure you don't want to come?"

Perry looked up from his communicator. "No I'm going to call my family, plus I don't want to run into Commodore Stellik again."

Skyler shrugged. "Be polite to the lady call her back, tell her she's too old for you. She gave you her contact."

Perry frowned. "You never call girls back."

Skyler grinned. "I tell them that, though. If they want to have another night out they got to call me. I don't like getting attached."

Perry looked up from his tablet. "For someone who doesn't like getting attached, you sure cling to your friends."

"Maybe I just have cute friends." Skyler made his way to the door. "Different types of relationships." He opened the door and made his way down the hall.

Kax was standing by the doors of the hall waiting.

"It's nice to see you again." Skyler strolled up beside her and leaned in to give her a kiss.

Kax playfully pushed him away. "Don't kiss me with that mouth. I know where it has been." She wiped her mouth.

Skyler stood back and laughed. "No fair. I know where your mouth has been, and I'm still willing to kiss you."

"You're not my boyfriend, so hands off." She teased him.

Skyler clenched his fist, imagining Kax and Commodore Kreeve together. "Right, I'm sorry, you like wrinkled cock."

Kax shot back. "And you like whore pussy."

Michael walked up to them and shook his head. "Could you two stop fighting? We are going to go out and have some fun, all right? Nothing to it. Let us not talk about our relationships tonight and have a fun night out."

Skyler smirked. "So Michael, are you finally going to get laid?"

Michael glared at Skyler. "You know the answer to that and 'no relationship talk' rule includes mine. Now let us go to the bar. I think I need a drink."

They made their way to the bar. Kax put in their drink order and came and joined them at the table. She sat down next to Michael and looked across at Skyler. "So, did you hear Cane is coming out here?"

Skyler's eyes picked up. "Really? When? How did you find out?"

"Well, my…" She paused and thought about Michael's rule about 'no relationships.' She thought, then continued. "One of my classmates told me."

Skyler knew where she got her source. "It will be great to see him again."

The drinks came. The waitress placed them on the table. Skyler gave her a tip.

Kax smiled. "I knew you would be happy."

Skyler took a sip of his beer. "I was going to call him but now that I know he is coming I will wait for him to show up."

Michael took a sip of his drink. "It probably has something to do with the war. He will not have time to talk or visit."

Skyler grinned. "He will have time for me."

Kax laughed. "I wouldn't doubt it." She turned to Skyler. "How is the situation on Earth going?"

Skyler played with his drink. "It's not great. The base is mostly closed. But there are attacks on earth at least once a week. They are moving a lot of our defenses to the closest base… which is?"

"The moon. They are trying their hardest to move the fight away from Earth to stop more people from being hurt. But it would appear all the Cass want is to hurt Earth," Michael said.

Skyler glared at Michael. "I know you know something about this war that only Squallites know. There are none here, so why don't you enlighten us?"

Michael took a sip of his drink. "Our conversations as friends have changed quite a lot, haven't they? I wish I knew the whole story but all I have ever been told is a Cass ship crashed on Squall years ago. The Squallites helped him on his way and the humans didn't. It seems petty to me but I am guessing the important details are what makes this a big deal. Because a group of Cass came by later and gave us the worm orb to say thank you."

Kax finished her drink. "We're going to war over an old vendetta?"

Skyler finished his beer. "That's usually how wars start. You piss off the wrong person and no one will take responsibility. Just, this is the third time they have gone to war with us, and I don't think it will be over soon."

Kax looked at Michael. "How is your dad doing with you not being home?"

Michael took a deep breath. "All right. They believe they have stopped the illness from spreading and he was sent back to duty full time on ships. He is fighting in this war but the good part is he is just repairing the ships on the ground. He will not be seeing any combat."

The waitress came by and gave them all refills on their drinks.

Skyler frowned. "How bad is Earth for the civilians, Kax? Your dad just came from there, will he be allowed to go back?"

Kax looked down at her drink and paused. "I'm not sure. I didn't talk to him about it. I assume he will be staying here for a few weeks but if the whole family is here, he might just stay with my brother and sister for a while."

Skyler's eyes widened. "Staying with you sister?"

"Yup," Kax laughed, "I guess you will have to break up with her."

Skyler shook his head, "I think your dad approves more of me dating your sister than the guy you're dating. You will have to break up."

Kax glared at Skyler.

Michael cut in. "Sorry but what was the rule I said, 'no relationship talk.'"

"Sorry Michael it's kind of hard not talking about it." Skyler turned to Kax. "When you graduate do you plan to move out here?"

Kax shook her head. "No I don't. I want to stay with my ship, it's too dark here for me. How are you adjusting to it here?"

Skyler shook his head. "It's too dark, but I don't mind the glowing asteroids, that's neat. Only thing that really bugs me about this place is the round doors. What is with that?"

Kax laughed, "round doors are just our thing, there is nothing we can really do about that."

Michael bowed his head. "I do not like the low ceilings. I am getting a bald spot on my head and neck cramps."

Kax leaned over and gave Michael a hug, "I'm sorry us cats are so short."

Skyler laughed, "you're just getting old, that's all. There isn't a problem."

Michael snapped back, "well then look forward to this in two years."

Skyler scoffed, "I got good genes. I will not be going bald or grey for a long time."

Kax pouted her face. "Then I guess you will have to wait for me a little longer."

Skyler's eyes widened. "Well who knows, I could take after my mom's side and get some grey very soon."

Michael laughed and finished his drink. "That was my second drink. I am going to turn in for the night."

Skyler frowned. "No you're not. You seem to keep drinking two and leaving. Stay a bit more. Our night has just begun."

Michael pointed to the fine print on the menus. "It says right here 'two drink minimum' so I come here, have my two drinks, go and sleep. I can not stay out all night. I have to get to work around 4 a.m. every day, I cannot stay out. Look at it this way, if I leave now you and Kax can talk about your relationships."

"Really, you have to get up that much earlier? What are you doing, prepping the plants? Before me and Perry get there?" Skyler asked, finishing his beer.

Michael nodded. "Exactly. James and I need to switch the lights and get the water on and check the plants. Before we begin work for the day. You know there are more than just the ones we have been working with in there. I am working there so I need to do all the work. It is hard work. Some plants are on timers but others need to be changed and monitored because we water them."

Kax frowned. "But 4 a.m.? When do you have time to rest? When does Dr. Fogg sleep?"

Michael counted the hours on his fingers. "I get about five hours of meditation and James actually sleeps in the back room of his office. He is never far from his plants."

Skyler frowned. "He must really love his plants."

Michael nodded. "He does, they are his passion."

Kax moved out of her seat. "Go on Michael, go get some rest. Thanks for coming out."

Michael took some money out of his pocket and placed it on the table. "This is for my drinks. Thanks for the time out. I will see you in the morning." He slid out of the booth.

Kax got back in her seat. "See you later, Michael. Sleep well."

Michael waved to both of them. "I will see you tomorrow."

Once he was gone Kax looked at Skyler and said, "you're going to dump my sister."

Skyler frowned. "Dump your boyfriend."

Kax glared at Skyler. "No, I like my guy and I think it could actually go somewhere. You and my sister, on the other hand, won't. You know she is just a casual girlfriend and she will drop you for the next best thing."

Skyler nodded. "She told me that but I want to see where this goes. You really think you could go somewhere with a man three times your age? He's older than your father and you won't even tell your father about him. I think I have a better chance with your sister."

Kax took a deep breath. "Even if what you say is true it bothers me you are with my sister."

"You're jealous, aren't you?" Skyler held up his hand. "Well it hurts me too that you're with this guy, but there's no ring on this finger. Until the day there is, I'm free to date whoever I want."

Kax took a deep breath. "Fine. Two can play it that way. I'm staying with my guy as long as I can then."

Damn this is making things worse. Skyler put on a phony smile. "I guess we have a deal. Both make our relationships last as long as possible, no matter what anyone says."

Kax held out her hand. "You got yourself a deal."

Skyler shook her hand firmly.

Chapter 12

There was a knock at the door. Skyler woke up rubbing his head. He put a pair of shorts on and answered the door with his eyes half open.

"Cadet Therris, do you have a hangover?"

Skyler rubbed his eyes and looked up. There was a big grin on his face when he saw whose stern voice it was. "Cane! You're here! Yes, I have a hangover. I went out partying with a girl last night." He gave Cane a big hug.

Cane hugged him back and ruffled his hair. "Is this girl serious?"

Skyler broke the hug and nodded. "Not really, it's more of a friend with benefits thing, her named is Kandice and she's Kax's sister." He walked into the room and put on his uniform pants. "Come in please."

Cane stepped into the room. "You know you have to clean this room up for inspection?"

Skyler zipped up his cadet jacket and looked around at the piles of clothes on the floor, "That's not 'til next week. I got lots of time to clean."

Cane shook his head and sat down on the bed. "That your roommate?" He pointed to the sleeping boy in the other bed.

Skyler nodded. "Yup, that's Perry Xyrik. He's my roommate here too."

Cane whispered. "I guess we should be quiet and not disturb him."

Skyler looked at the clock on the desk. "Hey Perry, get up! Time to get ready!" He hollered into his ear.

Perry jerked awake. "Dude, uncool! I hate it when you wake up first!"

Skyler laughed, "and how many times am I awake before you?"

Perry rubbed his eyes and looked to his side. "Cane, you're here? Why?"

Cane laughed. "You two bring back so many of my younger years. I'm here for Skyler. I was wondering if you would like to skip class and hang out with me for the day."

Skyler finished combing his hair. "I would love to, but aren't we in the middle of testing the new weapons?" He turned his attention to Perry.

Perry sat up in his bed. "We are, but I think if the fleet admiral wants you that means more than Dr. Fogg's orders."

Cane frowned. "Since when are you working with Dr. Fogg?"

Skyler popped a hangover pill into his mouth. "Dr. Fogg needed extra help with the bean guns and Michael volunteered me. I have been working weekends and before and after classes. Also I'm getting extra credit."

Cane shifted his eyes at the two boys. "I was not aware of this. I will have to look into it. The only two who are supposed to be working with Dr. Fogg are Michael and Perry. But don't worry about it. If the admiral here approved it, then I just missed it in my paperwork. But in any case, Skyler, you coming?"

Skyler nodded. "Any reason to hang out with you is worth it, sir."

Perry got out of bed and started putting on his uniform. "You two better have fun. Why am I always covering for you?"

Skyler grinned. "Because you love playing with plants."

Cane laughed. "Sorry Perry, I wish I could pull you out of class too but I have some things only Skyler can deal with."

Perry zipped up his cadet jacket. "It's no problem. You two bond." He looked at the clock. "Well, it looks like it is time for me to go." He finished with his uniform. "See you later." He walked out of the room.

Skyler smiled at Cane. "So, what are we going to do today?"

Cane laughed. "Paperwork. Well, I am. You are going to sit in my office, run errands for me and get me caught up on what has been going on."

Skyler laughed. "Seriously?"

Cane nodded. "I want to hang out with you and see how you have been doing. But every moment I have here is booked. The only way I can see you is to bring you on as my assistant."

Skyler sighed. "Well I guess it is better than playing with plants all day. Does this count as extra credit?"

Cane got up off the bed and headed to the door. "It will count for something. Come on Skyler, let's get some work done."

In the office Skyler sat down in front of Cane's desk. Cane sat down behind the desk.

Skyler looked around the office. "This room is just four walls and a desk. You're a fleet admiral shouldn't you have a bigger office than this?"

Cane nodded. "Yeah, well, at least they got a filing cabinet in here. I guess they gave me what they have in spare and don't expect me to have many guests."

Skyler made himself comfortable in the corner of the room. "So how long are you in town for?"

Cane looked at the calendar on his computer. "Two and a half weeks. Me and Davis are here. Davis will be staying and I will be sent to another post."

Skyler's eyes widened. "Why Davis and not Judson? Davis is a warlord."

Cane sighed. "It wasn't my choice. These were the orders of the King and the Minister of Defense. Davis is here to help get Catillion ready for battle. The Cass only know one thing and that is war, so it is the king's idea to outnumber them and prove that Earth has more allies then they can handle."

Skyler frowned. "You do know that this war is because of an old vendetta right?"

Cane nodded. "Yeah, but neither I or anyone alive on Earth is old enough to remember the cause of it. But since we can't talk to the Cass we have to force them into surrender."

Skyler rubbed his head. "I just hope it works."

Cane opened his desk drawer and pulled out a bottle of brandy, "I know it is way before noon, but want a drink?"

Skyler gave cane a thumbs up, "if we're going to keep talking like this I'm going to need booze."

Cane poured them both a glass and handed Skyler's to him. "Since the bottle is out, why does your mother keep calling the Earth Academy asking for you? Did you not tell her that you were getting posted here?"

Skyler took a big sip of his drink. "Nope, I didn't tell her and I got a new number."

Cane took a sip of his drink. He gave Skyler a stern look. "What's going on between you two?"

Skyler rubbed his temples. "She gave birth to a son and I left two days later. She wants me to quit, move back home and help her raise the brat. I have no intention of doing that. Her, Charles and the brat are a family and I have no plans of being involved with that."

"Makes sense. So what did they name the baby?" Cane asked.

He took a deep breath. "Phineas Adam Roux. I was there in the delivery room with my mom. She almost broke my hand."

Cane laughed. "Where was Charles?"

"Holding her other hand. We were both there."

Cane smiled. "Reminds me of when you were born. I was holding her other hand. I was there first. Your dad was busy doing captain stuff when your mother went into labor so I had to take her to the medical bay and page your father."

Skyler refilled his drink. "Really? Did my dad make it on time?"

"He did, and he was so proud when you were born. He hugged you and held you and never wanted to let you go. You were his. I held you and saw that you had the same sparkle in your eyes that he had. I knew you were destined for greatness." A tear came to Cane's eye.

"Wow, I never knew that." He took a sip of his drink.

Cane frowned. "You mean to tell me your mother never told you the story of your birth? You were your dad's good luck charm. We were on our way back from a mission and the Cassiopeans were going to attack us for being too close to them in the neutral zone. When Lord Jexloss realized that you had just been born, he called off the attack. Some sort of Cassiopean code. If it wasn't for you I know Lord Jexloss would have killed us. You saved the day."

Skyler turned his head to blush. "Really? I never knew that. My mom doesn't talk about my dad or my childhood much. I just have my dad's journals, logs and the memories of the stories he told me."

Cane narrowed his eyes. "Do you still have them? Did you bring them?"

Skyler nodded. "I have all my dad's stuff. When he died my mom put it all into boxes in the attic. I took the boxes when I moved out. She hasn't noticed."

Cane clenched his fists and let out a joyous cheer. "Skyler, can I look through those boxes? There are some things of your father's that have been missing for years and the info and items would be greatly helpful right now."

Skyler nodded. "I haven't taken them to my room yet. They're in the base's storage unit."

"What's your locker number?"

Skyler pulled out his card. "Unit 56B."

Cane typed it in and got on his intercom. "This is Fleet Admiral Cane. Could you bring up the entire contents of storage locker 56Beta?"

The voice on the other side replied. "Yes sir, and where would you like us to deliver it?"

Cane looked around his small office. "To the male dorm room 349."

The voice replied. "Yes sir. We will have it there as soon as possible."

Cane looked back up at Skyler. "Come on, let's go to your room and have a look at those boxes."

Skyler got up from his chair. They both made their way back to Skyler's room.

They didn't have to wait long before the boxes showed up. One by one the crew delivered the boxes into the room. Cane thanked them when they were done.

Cane looked at the boxes and frowned. "Were these the boxes you had under your bed back on Earth?"

Skyler nodded. "Yup, that's them. Some of them are my dad's stuff, the rest is mine."

Cane counted the boxes. "Nine medium square boxes. This isn't all your dad's stuff."

Skyler frowned. "What do you mean? This is all that was at my mom's house."

Cane shook his head. "There are some big items that would not fit in these boxes. But that's fine. What I need should be in the smaller stuff." Cane sat on Skyler's bed.

Skyler sat on the floor and opened the box with green tape on it. "This one is all his journals and logs. I have read them all."

Cane reached down and picked up a book and looked inside. "I wouldn't doubt it with your knowledge. But then you should have known the story of your birth? I saw your dad write that in his journal."

Skyler shook his head. "These only go up to 135GA, that's just before he met my mother."

Cane sighed and shook his head. "That explains a lot. Your father always kept a journal and he never stopped."

Skyler pulled out one of the purple leather bound books. "I have all his handwritten logbooks. Every year is here and—" he opened a green taped box. "Here. Half of this box is the rest of the logs. The rest is other things I could fit in there."

Cane reached down and grabbed the small wooden box off the top of the books and opened it. He smiled when he saw what was inside. He pulled out a small green pocket watch, "I remember when your dad got this. The metal is green and it only works on one planet. Your dad didn't care. He said, 'I want it and it matches my uniform.' He bought it and couldn't use it once we left. He tried many times to find someone to make it work but it still doesn't work."

Skyler opened the box with blue tape. "You know, I thought that was just a tarnished old watch, what planet does it work on?"

"Squarka, but nobody goes there. We needed an emergency repair one day and stopped. It's toxic to humans but the natives live fine." He looked at the box Skyler had just opened. "Does that wooden box contain what I think it contains?"

Skyler smiled and handed Cane the small wooden box, "It's exactly what you think."

Cane opened the box and pulled out a stone. "The Corsair Star. I'm surprised your mother didn't sell this. She could have, you could too."

Skyler nodded. "I won't sell it. It's too rare and it meant a lot to my father. As I see it, if it was my father's, it passes on to me."

Cane examined the stone. "You're right, it does, but you're a long way away from being a corsair. One day you could be." He handed the stone back.

Skyler put the box to the side. "Is there anything specific that you are looking for?"

"Yes I'm looking for a soft toy he gave you." Cane paused for a moment. "Are your father's medals in there?"

Skyler shook his head. "No I have no idea where they are. I only ever saw them on his uniform."

"Sandy has to know where the rest of the stuff is," Cane mumbled.

Skyler pulled out the stuffed spaceship and handed it to Cane. "Be careful that's my ship. Sorry I didn't wash it."

Cane could see the sentimental attachment Skyler had to this little stuffed space ship from when he was a small child. He squished the toy in his hands, feeling around for something. "Found it! Skyler, your father hid a key in here to something very valuable. Is it okay if I cut it open and take the key out?"

Skyler's eyes filled with worry. "Don't ruin it."

Cane looked at the toy and saw the added stitching. "Here is the spot your dad cut. I will just open the stitching and take the key out and stitch it back up."

Skyler grabbed the little ship. "I will do it!" He leaned over to his top desk drawer and pulled out a small pocket knife. Carefully and slowly he cut the stitches. He felt around and pulled out the key. He handed it to Cane. "What does this key open?"

Cane looked at the small tiny brass key. "I'm not 100% sure. I have to check the log to know. It is supposed to open something inside something else, I believe. Your father gave you the key for safe keeping. I knew it had to be in one of your toys and I have been trying to find it."

Skyler put his toy ship on his desk. "Why didn't you ask for it sooner?"

Cane looked down at the boxes of stuff. "You stopped playing with it when I was around and I wasn't sure where to look. Honestly I had much bigger things on my plate. Your father left me with a long list of things to do when he was gone."

Skyler looked up at Cane. "Did my dad often think about death?"

Cane looked into Skyler's weary eyes. "In our line of work death is always on our minds. But he didn't expect to die for a long time. His plan was when you were older to travel the stars with you at his side. Your father and I went on many missions together and we did some risky crazy things together. A lot of things were never completed." A tear came to Cane's eye. "This brings back so many memories."

Skyler opened the box with red tape on it. He pulled out a small green leather-bound book with gold trim. He handed it to Cane. "You can have this if you would like."

Cane looked at the book curiously. He took the book and opened it to the first page and began to cry. "Your father's photo album. Now this truly brings back memories." He flipped through the pages. "Surprised your mother didn't hide this one, since you and her are in it."

Skyler scratched his head. "I don't think she realized what it was."

Cane flipped through a few of the pictures, "I will definitely borrow this." He looked at the boxes again. "So if all these boxes are your dad's stuff, which ones have your stuff in them?"

Skyler put his hands on the two with yellow tape. "These ones. When you don't have a home you don't get to have a lot of stuff."

Cane frowned. "What do you mean by that?"

Skyler sighed. "You know when I was 16 Charles kicked me out of the house. I wasn't allowed back and then I spent the next two years at my uncle's and then here. I got no permanent place. What you see in this room is all I got."

Sorrow filled Cane's heart. "But what about the cabin? I thought you bought it last year?"

Skyler shook his head. "I had my uncle buy it for Kax. She loves the place and we needed somewhere to stay. But it's not my home. I can stay there when I want but this dorm room is the closest I have until I get my own ship."

"And you can't go back to your mom's house?"

Skyler shook his head. "Not as long as Charles is there. When I went back last winter he turned my room into an office, which is probably a nursery now. He has told me many times if I come back there he'll shoot me. My mom is the only one who wants me back there."

Cane clenched his fists. "I hate Charles so much for the things he has done to you. He was never a nice guy the times I met him."

Skyler looked through the box again and pulled out a small spire cut pendant wrapped in red wire. The blue gem had rune-like characters carved into it. "Hey Cane, what does this mean?"

Cane's eyes widened and he grabbed it out of Skyler's hand. "That son of a bitch!" He looked at Skyler and smiled. "Your father told me he never took one but he did. This is a key from Sergeion. It's their language on the sides. This is a key from the temples. Only certain people get these keys and they open a certain kind of storage lockers. Your dad wanted one but they wouldn't give him one. It looks like he stole it! I wonder what it opens. Your dad had a really bad habit of not listening to the rules."

A ringing sound came from Cane's communicator. He reached into his pocket. "Hello." He paused. "Okay I'll be right there." He turned off the communicator and got up off the bed, "Memory lane will have to be put on pause. We have work to do."

Skyler closed the boxes and pushed them under the bed quickly. "What are we doing?"

Cane left the album on the bed. "I have to talk to the admiral here about a few things. When we're in the meeting don't speak. You are just following me around and you know how Davis can be."

Skyler nodded in agreement. He followed Cane down the hall and through the buildings until they got to the meeting room.

There was a large round table in the center of the cylinder-shaped room. Red carpet covered, the floor and the walls were tan colored.

Cane took one of the red velvet seats at the round table.

Skyler sat down next to him.

Admiral Ciccone and Fleet Admiral Davis were already waiting.

Davis glared at Skyler. "Why is there a cadet here?"

"Rule number 347, fleet admirals are allowed to bring along one assistant of their choice at any time if they feel they are needed. Regardless of rank or status."

Admiral Ciccone responded. "Also rule 253, one outsider of the fleet admiral's choice is allowed to sit in on a meeting of such importance."

Davis grumbled. "Fine but he better be quiet and not interfere with the rest of the meeting."

Skyler pursed his lips.

Cane gave it a few seconds. "Okay so if everyone is ready what is this meeting about?"

Admiral Ciccone spoke. "I have called you two here to talk about the war and what the status of this base is. I want to make sure all things are clear and this deal is still in the best interest for everyone."

Cane and Davis both nodded.

"You may proceed," Davis said.

Admiral Ciccone began to speak. "Right now, we are helping you develop weapons for your war with the Cass, because the specialist for this is on this planet. He is doing this to work off time on his sentence. We hold him here because he was banned from your galaxy and Earth provides us protection from our own enemies. But doing that isn't enough. You want Catillion to go to war as well in another galaxy. Not only does it take a while to get to the battle but we also don't have that many ships. Why is this a good idea for us?"

Cane spoke up, "we have the worm orb and you can use it to make the journey from here to Earth or any planet in a matter of seconds. We will still defend your planet from the Doallion. Catillion will not be harmed. We just need to show the Cass we have strong allies."

Admiral Ciccone shook his head. "How do you plan to defend your planet and ours when you're fighting a war? If we move our ships to help you the Doallion will know and attack us as well as the Cass. We can build your weapons and we can supply you units but we cannot fight."

"We are not asking you to fight or leave your planet defenseless. Half the ships in your fleet will be enough to prove to the Cass," Cane said.

Davis spoke up, "we need more than half. The Doallion are no threat to you. You can afford to spare more of your army. If you don't believe us we will give you three ships of ours to watch your planet. With the new alloy we have our ships are stronger. We would be willing to share that with you if you assist us in this war."

Admiral Ciccone smiled. "I think we can work something out." He pulled out some documents out of the folder he held in front of him. He took a pen and passed it to Cane.

Skyler spoke up. "In the last year we have made five ships completely with the new alloy and they are on the frontlines right now. Davis you want to take three of the best warships we have and give them to the Catillions? Or are you referring to the ten ships that have the alloy plating, which doesn't cover it all and they are considered just slightly better warships?"

Admiral Ciccone took back his paperwork. "Is this true?"

Davis glared at Skyler. "How do you know how many ships we have?"

Skyler grinned. "My roommate and good friend invented the alloy that is now being used on these ships. He is here on this planet now working on the new weapons you were talking about earlier."

Admiral Ciccone shifted his eyes. "The man who invented Jonesium is the same guy we have working in the greenhouse?" He smirked. "Well now it appears I have a genius stationed on this base. When was Earth going to tell me this?"

Cane responded, "Yes he is here only to apprentice with Dr. Fogg. Once he is done he will be sent back to Earth."

Admiral Ciccone pulled out his tablet and found Michael's file. He read it over quickly, "I don't think so. He is too valuable. I think we might just hold on to him. It's in his contract. He is here until he is no longer needed. It does not say until the weapons are made. I think we can find other things for him to be needed in."

Cane spoke up, "Cadet Jones is my cadet. My men sent him here to make these weapons and that is it. You cannot hold Cadet Jones hostage!"

Skyler got up out of his chair and turned on the screen in the center of the table and pulled up statistics of both planets' ships and weapons. "He won't be holding anyone hostage when he sees this."

Cane whispered to Skyler, "you better know what you're doing kid."

Skyler picked up the pointer stick off the console and pointed to the map. "The Doallion have not attacked Catillion in almost three years. That is not because of Catillion's defenses but because of the asteroid field. If you take into account they lost 1/3 of their ships last war just from being hit by that seemingly unpredictable asteroid field, I don't think they will be coming back anytime soon. But if you want to attack them, there is one guy I know who can predict the asteroid's movement better than your weathermen."

Admiral Ciccone frowned. "Who can predict the asteroids? They're so erratic. We have been trying for centuries,"

Skyler smiled. "I don't know how but Dr. Fogg knows more about them than the weathermen. We have contests when working with the plants who's right and he always gets it on the dot."

Admiral Ciccone's eyes widened. "Are you serious? He has only been here for five years. That's impossible."

Skyler shrugged. "I have no idea how he does it but you can talk to him." He pointed to another part of the map. "You figure out the patterns of the asteroids, move through them and easily attack or occupy their planet. You have the firepower now to attack them and probably win. Now with your issues of going to war with the Cass, you just need to look like you are going to fight. So bring your defensive ships to the battlefield and hold on. You don't need to fight, but if you do end up fighting, you will have the firepower. The Cass have no beef with you so they will most likely not attack you unless desperate. You can carry out these two wars at once if you wanted, leaving your planet's only defense the asteroids that surround it—which is a pretty good defense system already. Any questions?"

All three of them looked astonished at Skyler.

Davis frowned. "Are you sure you're a cadet?"

Skyler nodded his head. "I sure am, fourth year advanced command."

Davis focused her attention on Cane. "You got one smart cadet."

Admiral Ciccone nodded. "Well, if what the boy is saying is true then I have no problem working this deal out. But I want Cane here instead of Davis as the fleet admiral on base."

Skyler turned his head and looked at Cane with hopeful eyes.

Cane put his head down. "Sorry but I can't do that. I am needed on Swopart."

Davis nodded her head. "Yes, and I chose this posting. I'm much more needed here."

Skyler's eyes became sad and weary-looking as if to be saying, 'Please, please, please.'

Cane's heart was breaking, *Damn it Skyler why are you doing this to me.* He took a deep breath. "Well I guess I could make some arrangements if that's what's it's going to take to get this deal to work."

Davis glared. "And where am I supposed to go? I need to train an army!"

Cane pulled out his tablet. He scrolled around and then said. "Squall, that's your other option. They're in the war already and aren't big fighters. Go there. We can talk to the minister of defense about it later. I was scheduled to be here for two weeks as it is so we can figure that out later."

Skyler smiled and took his seat next to Cane.

Admiral Ciccone turned the screen off. "Well then, if that's all settled I will adjourn this meeting."

They all stood up and made their way to the door.

Admiral Ciccone put his hand on Skyler's shoulder. "Cadet Therris, are you by any chance Captain Levi Therris's son?"

Skyler nodded. "Yes sir."

Admiral Ciccone rubbed his shoulder and smiled. "You're definitely his kid."

"Uh, thank you, sir," Skyler said.

Cane coughed, hinting to Skyler to go.

Skyler turned around and followed Cane out of the room.

Cane was silent until he got back to his office. He looked at Skyler. "Okay, what was that about? I told you to be quiet!"

Skyler looked down. "I'm sorry, sir. I just saw a better way to fix the situation."

Cane sat down at his desk and took a deep breath. "You did a good job and proved you knew what you were doing. I'm happy with the end results but I'm not happy about staying here."

Skyler frowned. "I thought you wanted to stay here?"

Cane poured a glass of brandy for him and Skyler, "I would like to stay here to keep an eye on you but I'm really needed on Swopart. I guess that will have to wait."

Skyler took his glass. "Can't you make a quick mission over there?"

Cane shook his head. "No what I need to do takes work and I will be working for a long time. It takes about a week to get there too. So even if I rushed it I would use up all my holidays. I will just have to push it back is all."

"I'm sorry Cane."

"It's not your problem, I'll figure it out." Cane said.

***

Perry was reading his tablet when Skyler came into the room. "It's almost 2 a.m." He looked up at Skyler. "You're still wearing your uniform. Where did you go?"

Skyler fell on his back on his bed. "I just got off from my day with Cane. We get to go to sleep now."

Perry laughed. "Well good news, I called my dad. He said my sister decided to join the academy this year, she was sent to Squall for her first year. But my dad is coming out to visit in two weeks. He will bring the newspaper articles he has about Dr. Fogg. He says it has got to be him."

Skyler got up and started taking his clothes off. "Oh ya, that's what I learnt for you today. Dr. Fogg is smart but he was banned from the Milky Way Galaxy and so he has been posted here in the Andromeada Galaxy."

Perry's eyes widened. "Really? He must really be an important asset to keep him alive. How did you find this out?"

Skyler rubbed his face, standing in the middle of the room naked. "Meeting with Cane. Too tired. Talk about it in the morning."

Perry looked at Skyler getting into bed. "Uh you're not wearing shorts tonight?"

"See something you like?" Skyler hopped into bed. "I hate wearing shorts." Skyler closed his eyes and went to bed.

Chapter 13

Michael was pruning one of the plants. He saw Skyler playing with his tablet. "Skyler, you can play with your tablet later."

Skyler frowned, "I'm trying to get ahold of Kax. I haven't heard from her since Saturday and it's Monday. I'm getting worried."

Michael frowned. "Come to think of it, I have not heard from her either or seen her. I wonder what is up."

Skyler checked his tablet one more time. "When I last saw her she was waiting to meet her boyfriend."

A looked of worry crossed Michael's face. "You know what? I will go talk to her. She may just not want to talk to you." He looked at the time. "It is close to lunch, she should be in her room. I will take lunch off and go stop by her room."

Skyler smiled and put his tablet down. "If something is wrong send me a message."

Michael nodded, "I will. Do not worry about that. Just tell James where I went for lunch." He made his way out of the greenhouse, across the courtyard and to Kax's dorm.

He knocked on the door. There was no reply. He knocked again, nothing. He talked to the door. "Kax it is Michael, no one has seen you in days. If you are in there, open up." He waited.

A moment later the door opened up a crack. Kax's hair was a mess. There were bruises on her face.

He slid his foot in the door, preventing her from closing it. "Kax, what happened to you?"

She tried to close the door and ran to her bed and cried.

Michael entered the room, closed the door behind him. "What happened to you?" He sat on the end of the bed.

She lifted her head off the pillow. "Skyler was right. That's what I hate about this."

Michael sat down on the bed. "Right about what?"

She sat up. "Kreeve raped me. He thought I was cheating on him with Skyler, because he saw us kiss. He saw Skyler leave my room and thought I slept with him. I told him Skyler was just a friend and so he-"

"Raped you?" Michael cut. The fire burned in his eyes.

She cried into her hands.

Michael gripped his fist in rage. "That bastard! I will make him pay and kill him!"

Her eyes widened. "No, you can't. If you do I might lose my career over it."

He glared. "Kax, he forced himself on you. That is rape and I will not tolerate that!" His eyes flashed with rage.

She put her arms around Michael. "Not yet! Please let me talk to him. Maybe we can work something out. He isn't a bad guy."

Michael pushed her off him. "He is a bad guy. Why are you defending him?"

She wiped a tear from her eye. "Because I'm scared he will do worse and that I will be kicked out for being with him."

Michael stood up. "Fine, let us get you cleaned up. Have you eaten? I will tell Skyler about this and you are going to have to convince him not to report this."

Kax got up off the bed. "So you're not going to report this?"

Michael shook his head. "No, you are going to report him. But right now we are going to get you cleaned up. Cane knows you are a good pilot. I do not think they are going to kick you out. He is the criminal here. But let's get you cleaned up. There are cameras in the hallways. I wonder if there will be footage of him coming and going in your room."

She grabbed her hairbrush and started brushing her hair. She winced when she hit the bump.

Michael took the brush from her hand and brushed her hair very carefully. "Your head is probably going to be sore for a few more days. I will be gentle." He fixed her hair. She got some clothes out of her drawer.

Michael waited outside the door as she got dressed. She came out a moment later. Michael snapped a photo of her face and neck.

She frowned. "What did you do that for?"

"Evidence, in case they heal quick." He walked with her down to the cafeteria. They both grabbed fruit cups and salad.

"Michael, can we go back to the room? Everybody is looking at me."

He shook his head. "Eat your food. We got to go see Cane next."

She shook her head. "No I'm not reporting him yet." She chewed a piece of fruit. It hurt to swallow.

"Your throat hurts still. Go to the doctor and get this written down. We can talk to him about your options."

She did her best to eat some food with the pain.

Michael texted Skyler and told him in brief what happened.

She looked up at Michael. "Did you just text Skyler?"

Michael nodded. "I told you I would. He is very worried about you."

She looked down at her plate. "He probably thinks I'm weak letting this happen to me."

Michael shook his head. "I do not think he does. You are a victim. You cannot win every battle. You have seen how good I am in hand to hand combat. Well, that took lots of practice. I used to get beat up all the time when I was a kid for being a Squallite. I hated going to school. Then I learnt if I took on extra classes and kept my nose in a book I would have less time to be around bullies. Only once I joined the Forces did they make me fight."

Kax tried to smile with her swollen face. "I guess I will just have to learn to protect myself better."

"Talk to Skyler, he got beaten by his step-dad a lot. He might have some tips."

She thought about it. "I did not realize. I mean I think he has mentioned it to me but I never put much thought into it."

Michael finished his food. "Your choice, who do you want to go see first, Cane or the doctor?"

Kax sat there playing with her piece of fruit. "I don't know yet. I guess the doctor, but I do want to talk to Skyler."

Michael picked up their trays. "I will send a message to Skyler to meet us at the doctor's office."

She shook her head. "I don't want to be seen in public with him. Can I go to the greenhouse with you?"

Michael thought about it. "Dr. Fogg does not really want anyone else there but I think in this case he will let you in." He got up and took the trays to the garbage.

She followed him all the way to the greenhouse. She tried to use her hair to cover the purple bruises on her face.

Michael pinned in his passcode and walked into the greenhouse.

***

Skyler was waiting for Kax in the greenhouse. He saw her and hugged her tight. "I'm so sorry he did this to you. I will kill him and make sure he can never hurt you or anyone else."

She pushed away from him. "Don't kill him Skyler, that's horrible."

He looked at the marks on her face, brushing her hair aside and examining her face and neck. He closed his eyes trying not to cry. "I never wanted this to happen to you."

She turned her face away from him. "Skyler, is there a quiet place where we can talk?"

He looked around. He took her hand. "Ya, come on." He walked with her to one of the climate rooms. He grabbed the chair from outside and brought it into the room.

He sat on the stool and gave her the nice chair. "So what do you want to talk about?"

She played with her hands, and looked down. "Michael told me Charles used to beat you."

Skyler took a deep breath and looked down. "Yup, from the age of 12 until he threw me out at 16, and even over last winter break. Whenever my mother wasn't home he took a swing at me. I got a few fractured ribs and a bunch of times I looked worse than you."

She looked up at him. "Did he ever rape you?"

Skyler was taken back by the comment. "No, there where a few times I think he wanted to. But just punching, kicking, hair pulling. Why, did Kreeve rape you?"

She put her head down.

Skyler's eyes popped from his skull. "He did what? I will kill him for that!" He made a fist. "I'll give that bastard something to choke on."

Kax put her hand on Skyler's knee. "No not yet. I want to talk to you first. He did it because he thought I was cheating on him with you."

Skyler's heart sunk and a tear came to his eye. "Oh Kax, don't say that. I never meant to cause you harm. I never meant to be the bad guy."

Kax shook her head and went up the Skyler and hugged him. "No, he is the bad guy here It is not your fault. I told him the truth and he is the one who refused to believe it. Skyler, you are a good friend and in no way caused this. It was my own stupidity."

Skyler brushed her hair back and kissed her on the forehead. "You're not stupid, it is not your fault. Come on, let's get you to a doctor. I could never report Charles because of his job but you can report this guy. You will regret it if you don't."

She held on to Skyler tight. "Okay, I'll go with you."

They got out of the room. Dr. Fogg was waiting for them. "Friends aren't allowed in here. Not my rule; it's one of my probation conditions."

Skyler had his arm around Kax's shoulders and looked up at Dr. Fogg. "I'm sorry, sir, it won't happen again, but I got to take my friend to the doctor now."

Dr. Fogg leaned down and looked at Kax's face. "Commodore Kreeve did this, right?"

Kax nodded.

Dr. Fogg tickled her ear. "Come back here when you're done. I have something for you."

Kax nodded and started to walk away with Skyler. Fogg grabbed Skyler's shoulder and whispered into his ear. "Go to the Cat Scratch bar tonight or tomorrow. You have to go there, trust me."

This is not the time to be talking about picking up women, Skyler thought to himself, "Okay sir, see you later."

Skyler walked with Kax down the hall, leaving Michael and Perry to do their work.

***

Kax and Skyler waited in the doctor's office.

Kax was sitting on the bed of the small room. When the doctor came in, she introduced herself. "Hello I am Dr. Tills. What seems to be the issue?"

Kax moved her hair away from her face. "My boyfriend raped me. I need to put it on record."

Dr. Tills looked around the room and saw Skyler sitting down in the chair. "Is this your boyfriend?"

Skyler raised his hands backing off. "No, I'm a good friend, and I would like to say I would never lay a hand on a woman. I want to kill the asshole who did this."

Kax frowned. "Skyler calm down." She looked at the doctor. "I do want to report this but not yet. I want to talk to someone else before this report is submitted."

The doctor frowned. "Who do you wish to speak to?"

"Fleet Admiral Cane. He is a friend of ours."

Dr. Tills nodded. "I can do the report now and send a copy right to Cane. So he can know what is going on when you talk to him?"

Skyler nodded. "That would be good."

Kax nodded her head in agreement.

Dr. Tills nodded and pulled up the form on her tablet. "First I need the name of who did this to you."

Kax took a deep breath. "Commodore Kreeve. He is my flight instructor and we had been seeing each other in secret for the last couple of months."

She wrote some things down on the tablet. "He was the one who raped you?"

Kax nervously responded. "I know it was illegal but I liked him, he liked me."

Dr. Tills asked again. "What exactly happened?"

Kax nodded. "He came into the room and accused me of cheating on him and started to attack me." Tears began to fill her eyes, she paused trying not to think of it. "Grabbed my hair. Threw me on the floor. I banged my head and then he grabbed me by the hair again. Slapped me a few times then and pulled out his…" She started to cry.

Skyler got up out of his chair and sat on the bed next to her. He put his arm around her rubbing her shoulder. "Don't worry about it, just tell her, okay? Tell her what happened. He can't hurt you no more."

She took a moment and picked her head up. With tears rushing down her face she finished telling her story.

Skyler held her close. "It's okay, you will be fine now. The doctor will take care of it."

She finished typing in the report. "Skyler could you please get off the bed? I need to examine Kax now."

Skyler gave Kax a kiss on the forehead and jumped down from the bed and went back to his chair.

Dr. Tills touched Kax's head checking for bruises, cuts and other damage. She then looked at the bruises on Kax's face and neck. She looked in Kax's throat. She examined the rest of her body and wrote down all her findings. She sat back down and said, "I'm going to send this report to Fleet Admiral Cane and tell him to come down here immediately."

Kax nodded. "I'm not in trouble, am I?"

Dr. Tills looked at the report. "I'm not the one who decides that, but in my opinion as a doctor you are the victim. You have done nothing wrong."

Skyler went back to sitting next to Kax. He comforted her while they waited for Cane to show up. He entered the room trying to look professional even if he was clearly out of breath. He looked around the room and saw Kax, Dr. Tills and Skyler. "I came as soon as I got the report." He looked at Kax. "Kax, there are a few questions I'm going to ask you. I know you would never lie to me so don't take these questions as attacks. I have to ask them, do you understand?"

Kax nodded. "Yes I understand."

Cane stood in front of her and asked her. "You said Commodore Kreeve raped you, is that true?"

Kax cried. "Yes."

Cane asked her another. "In the time you and him were together, did he rape you then or is this the first time?"

Kax's hand shook. "He has been rough but never raped me."

Cane nodded. "Okay, that's good for now."

Kax looked up at him with her big eyes. "Am I in trouble for dating him?"

Cane took a deep breath. "As it stands, no. I don't know for certain yet. We have to look into this case further. You can still continue your studies."

Kax's eyebrows raised. "No, I can't go back to class with him."

"You don't have to worry, now that you have submitted this report, Commodore Kreeve is on suspension until we get to the bottom of this." He thought for a second. "Do you have any evidence that can prove you two were together?"

She shook her head, "no we didn't give gifts or anything. But my sister has seen him come into my room, she knew about the relationship. But he always came to my room, you can check the security tapes."

Cane nodded. "I will definitely check into that. Anything else?"

Skyler spoke up. "I saw her giving him a blow job once under his desk during lunch hour."

Cane's eyes widened. "Well then I think that will be enough to get this case off the ground." His eyes saddened. "Kax, return to class when you're ready, don't force yourself. Take a few days off as needed."

Kax nodded. "Yes sir, thank you sir."

"Well I must be off now." He saluted them and then left the room.

Chapter 14

Dr. Fogg watched Perry pruning some of the plants. "Perry, do you have a problem with me?"

Perry didn't turn around and just said. "Why would you say that?"

Dr. Fogg put his hand on Perry's shoulder and watched him flinch. "Because you did that. You use to be so cheery when you saw me. You were like a younger me when it came to plants."

Perry turned around. "I'm not like you and I will never be like you!"

Dr. Fogg stepped back. "Perry come see me in my office."

Perry followed Dr. Fogg to the office. He sat down in the chair.

Dr. Fogg sat down behind his desk and said. "Okay Perry, what's wrong? You seem to have an issue with me."

Perry took a deep breath. "I'm from Colony H…"

Dr. Fogg frowned. "What's that have to do with anything? I was never there."

Perry frowned. "No but you were on Colony J. My uncle lived there. I know what you did to the people, the people you killed with your plants."

"I see." Dr. Fogg nodded. "You're right, I did do that and that's why I'm here. Perry, you must understand I didn't want to kill those people. I killed them because I spent so much time getting their plants to grow so they could have food and they chose not to listen to my instructions on how to take care of the plants. They did their own thing and the plants were going to die. I didn't want to see my plants die so I sent some poisonous flowers and their gas killed everyone. The people would have died anyway in the year if I let them just ruin the plants. I don't know how the other colonies treated them, because I just sent the plants to the others I didn't terraform them."

Perry nodded. "You wiped out an entire colony!"

Dr. Fogg bowed his head. "I can't say I'm sorry about it. I did what I felt was right at the time. That's one of the reasons I'm here. After Captain Therris caught me smuggling, they sent me to work in many different areas involving plants. Then the incident happened. I know the only reason they kept me alive was because of my brain and talents."

Perry stared dead into his eyes. "My uncle was on Colony J and you killed him along with his wife and child. He was a surgeon. He had nothing to do with your plants."

Dr. Fogg put his head down. "I'm sorry for your loss. But Perry I want you to know I did what I felt was right. You can hate me for it but I wish you would put it behind you. My actions were my own and in the past." He raised his head and looked straight at Perry. "I was going to talk to you about this before. I hope you will still consider my offer. Perry, you have an amazing talent with the plants and you have a rare passion and skill. I wish for you to continue working with me. Michael is good but he is just smart, he doesn't have the passion. When this is done, you could join me and become my personal apprentice."

Perry's eyes widened. His hands shook. "Uh, wow! I don't know what to say. If you would have told me before I would have jumped at this opportunity, but now it doesn't seem right."

Dr. Fogg smiled. "Take your time. This offer will always be open to you. But it would mean a permanent move to Catillion. I can't leave this galaxy and there aren't many bases outside of the Milky Way but it is something to think about."

Perry looked down. "Permanent? I really will have to think about that. I wanted to move back to Colony H when I was finished. That's my home."

"Home is something I can never go back to. If you can, I would not want to take that from you."

Perry frowned. "Where is your home?"

Before Dr. Fogg could answer he got up from his seat. "Looks like your friends Kax and Skyler are back." He went to the door. "Skyler, you're back! Good to see you. How did things go?"

Skyler nodded. "The doctor checked her out did a few tests and we put in a report and talked to Cane."

Dr. Fogg's eyes widened. "Cane is here?"

Skyler frowned. "Ya, didn't Perry tell you last week when I took the day off?"

Perry shook his head. "I just said you were helping on assignment. I didn't mention Cane. I figured if your dad was the one who caught him he would not be excited to see Cane."

Dr. Fogg turned and looked at Perry. "I'm not afraid of Cane. He is my probation officer if you can call anybody that. It would be good to see him. Davis is the one I'm really scared of. Bitch hates plants. I gave her a bonsai once and she threw it in the trash. She is the one I want to stay away from."

Skyler laughed. "There are many who would agree with you. But you might get your wish. Admiral Ciccone wants to keep Cane here and send Davis to Squall."

Michael came over and said. "Do not send Davis to Squall. She cannot make soldiers out of the Squallites. They are not fighters."

Dr. Fogg's eyes lit up. "Let's fight this war with plants."

They all looked at him oddly.

"Uh you said to bring Kax here after we saw the doctor." Skyler said.

Dr. Fogg shook his head and returned to reality. "Yes come with me, miss. I have something for you."

Kax and Skyler followed Dr. Fogg who took them to a dark room in the back of the greenhouse. He turned on the ultraviolet light, walked in and went over to a plant that looked like a cactus but with bright red cherries growing all over it. He picked one and handed it to Kax. "Eat this."

She looked nervous but took a bite of it. "Ew, that tastes like fabric softener."

Dr. Fogg nodded. "That sounds about right but now how does your throat feel?"

She tried swallowing. "Not bad, thank you!"

"Oh it is not over yet. I got something else for your bruises." He took them out of the room and back into the main greenhouse. He grabbed a leaf off a yellow tree. He handed it to her. "Rub this anywhere there is a bruise."

She took the leaf and followed his instructions.

Skyler watched in amazement. "Wow that's taking off the bruises like an eraser. What kind of plants are these?"

Dr. Fogg smiled. "The first one is a type of cactus called a Kintalia and great for healing raw and damaged tissues, works great for colds as well. The second one is this tree is called a Hyucala tree. The bruises are still there but the residue on the leaves is a great healer and cover up."

Kax smiled. "You made these plants?"

Dr. Fogg shook his head. "No I collected them. They are from some strange parts of the galaxy. If you took the time you would find that all of my plants are helpful in some way. It's good to have at least one of everything in here."

Skyler looked around. "Do you have one of everything?"

Dr. Fogg shook his head. "Nowhere near. I wish I had more. But I don't get out often and There are some plants I'm not allowed to own or are yet to be discovered."

Kax smiled. "Thank you for your help doctor."

Dr. Fogg smiled. "Call me James." He went over to the side and picked up one of the seedlings on the shelf and brought it over to her. "Here, you can have this little guy. He will look nice in your room."

She took the little green seedling. "What kind of plant is it?"

He smiled. "That is a surprise. But I will give you a set of instructions to take care of it. Make sure you follow them to the letter. Do not kill this plant. I don't know how long you will be here for but when you do have to leave either pass the plant on or give it back to me."

Kax played with the leaves. "I will. Thank you James. I will take care of this little one."

Skyler snickered at Kax and the plant.

James frowned at Skyler. "What is so funny?"

"Keeping plants like they're pets or humans. They're just plants."

James' eyes bulged. "That's another strike. They're much more than just plants. A plant will do more than any pet and will live longer than any pet or human. They were here before us and they will be here after us."

Perry put his hand on Skyler's shoulder and whispered into his ear. "Take it back, don't insult plants near him."

Skyler awkwardly smiled. "It's a lovely gift and I'm sure Kax will take good care of it. You're right; plants are important."

James closed his eyes. He let out a kind smile. "You have got a lot to learn."

***

Skyler walked Kax back to her room. "You sure you're going to be okay?"

Kax sighed. "I will be okay, it just feels weird going back to my room."

Skyler took a deep breath. "If you want to come to my room, you can. Perry is going to be out all night working with the plants. His bed will be free."

Kax looked down at the little plant in her hand. She looked back up at Skyler. "Sure, we can do that."

Skyler walked with Kax to the other building where his dorm was. He opened the door for her. For once he noticed how messy the room was. There were shirts all over the floor. The beds were unmade. There was even a pair of her sister's panties on the end of his bedpost. He quickly ran in front and kicked the clothes under the bed and grabbed the panties, placing them in his pocket. He threw the blanket over his bed. He smiled and said. "Sorry about the mess."

She laughed and placed her little plant on the desk. "Skyler I have known you for about four years. I know what your room looks like on non-inspection days."

Skyler covered his face. "Sorry I'm a slob."

She sat down on his bed. "No need to apologize."

Skyler sat down next to her. He looked out the window. "You know with the long periods of darkness I have to look at a clock to know if it is late or not."

Kax laughed. "Skyler I just want to get some sleep right now if that's okay with you."

Skyler nodded. "Ya let's get to bed." He looked at her clothes, she was still wearing her t-shirt and blue jeans. He went over to the closet and pulled out Perry's robe. He then walked over to the dresser at the end of his bed and pulled out a blue t-shirt and a pair of clean shorts. He gave them to Kax, "I'm sorry I should keep a set of women's clothes around more but I don't. I haven't worn this pair of shorts yet so you can have them and the shirt's new and that's Perry's robe."

She was flattered by the gesture. "Thank you Skyler. I guess I will put these on."

He turned away. "Well you don't have to wear them if you don't want to."

She smiled. "You went to the effort. I will put them on."

Skyler grabbed another pair of shorts out of the drawer. He turned his back to the wall. "I'm going to get changed. I won't look. We can both do it at the same time."

She lightly smiled. "Okay sounds good to me."

Skyler turned around, took off his pants and slowly put on his shorts. He picked up his pants, folded them and put them on top of his dresser. He then unzipped his cadet jacket and pulled it off. Folded it and placed it on top of his pants. He was now just wearing his green shorts and black undershirt. He waited a moment then said. "Are you done?"

"Just about." She said.

Then they turned around together.

Skyler laughed when he saw Kax in his t-shirt and shorts. "You look hilarious. Never wear guy's underwear again unless you got something to put in them."

She frowned and headed to the bed and got in.

Skyler walked over to Perry's bed.

She rolled over. "Skyler, isn't this your bed?"

Skyler nodded. "It is."

"Well then come sleep in it. I am still upset and I want someone who can relate to me to comfort me. Please just cuddle."

Skyler's heart raced, *Kax wants to share my bed with her. Damn I wish she wasn't so upset; this could be a dream come true.* He shook his head. *No I can't do that even if she wants it she's too upset right now.* He knew how many nights he had just wanted to cuddle with someone and have someone tell him it would be alright. He got up and turned the desk lamp on, and went to the door and turned off the light. He walked over to his bed and hopped into bed with Kax. He rolled over, turned the desk lamp off and put his arm around Kax, holding her close. He whispered into her ear, "Everything is going to be alright."

He spooned her holding her close. Making her feel safe in his arms.

She whispered back, "thank you." She then closed her eyes and went to sleep.

He held her for a bit, enjoying the moment they were sharing together. But he was worried, *What if Kax wakes up and freaks out we're in bed together? Or that I have morning wood?* He waited a bit more. *When she is in a deep sleep, I will go to Perry's bed. She won't notice.*

He laid on his back staring up at the ceiling when the door opened.

Perry walked in and saw Skyler in bed with Kax. "All right dude, good for you."

Skyler shook his hands. He put his finger over his mouth and went 'shhh.' Skyler got out of the bed slowly and dragged Perry into the hall. "Kax didn't want to go to her room. She is wearing my clothes and just wanted to be comforted. Nothing happened with us. By the way I lent her your robe. I thought you were working on plants all night?"

"I left shortly after you and took the night off, long story." Perry frowned. "You gave her my robe? What am I supposed to wear after my morning shower?"

Skyler frowned. "Your towel. Borrow mine if you have to. Kax needed it more." He noticed Perry didn't smell like alcohol. "Where were you?"

Perry smiled. "I called Commodore Stellik back. She is really nice. I think I like her."

Skyler laughed. He patted Perry on the back. "She's almost as old as your mom. But let's get back into the room and be quiet." They walked back into the room. Skyler hopped into Perry's bed.

Perry took off his uniform. Turned around and saw Skyler. He whispered. "Your bed is over there, sleep in there."

Skyler shook his head. "I don't want Kax to freak out, and you know urges, morning wood. I can't control myself around her. She's like super Viagra."

Perry nodded and hopped into bed with Skyler. "We never speak of this and don't poke me."

Chapter 15

Dr. Fogg was sleeping in his back room when his alarm went off. He jerked out of bed and looked at his security screen. *I was wondering when you would show up.* He put on his lab coat and went to the main entrance to the greenhouse and smiled, "Lt. Cane nice to see you again."

Cane looked him over. "Does nobody like to put on pants anymore, and it is Fleet Admiral Cane. You know that, it's been over 10 years now."

Dr. Fogg smiled, "I know but I liked you back when you were a Lieutenant. You were so much more of a hardass. I think time has made you soft. Or is it Skyler?"

Cane glared. "Can I come in? I need to talk to you before I leave."

He stepped back from the door and let Cane in. He walked with him to his office. Dr. Fogg sat down at his desk. "Let's skip the formalities, I have no plans to run away and I am not planning to kill anyone."

Cane looked at the plants growing on the walls. "I'm more worried about your involvement with my cadets. You have become close to Jones, Therris and Zyrix. I'm just making sure you are not corrupting them and keeping things professional."

"And Tillion." James added.

Cane frowned. "What about Tillion? Her name wasn't on the list of students you are tutoring."

James smiled. "No, but she has been by and I'm getting to know her. It's a shame what happened to her with Commodore Kreeve, but I'm glad he is finally getting what's coming to him. Kax is not the first girl he has done this to."

Cane frowned. "We are not here to talk about the cadets, we are here to talk about you. What I need to know. What have you been up to since our last meeting?"

He raised his hands and smiled. "You see it. Plants—that's all I can do. They have me on house arrest. I have been told I have a nice apartment, but I have never seen it." He picked up his leg and placed it on the desk. "There's a flashing microchip in the bone on my ankle. After you left they put it there. I grow my own food and there is a lovely lady who takes my laundry once a week. I can go as far as the roof before an alarm goes off and a searing pain goes through my body."

Cane examined his ankle. "That's torture, you were supposed to stay away from the public not forced to live like a prisoner. What do you do for fun?"

Bowing his head, James said, "my days of fun are over. I love my plants and they keep me entertained. Michael is the first real visitor who I have had in years. I wish he could stay forever, or Perry, he is a real pleasure and he loves plants almost as much as me. I want a companion."

Cane frowned. "You want a male companion? That's your, um, preference."

James laughed. "Not like that. I want someone like the cadets I have now. I love their spunk and initiative. Also I'm not into guys or girls like that. As it says on my file I'm an objectophile and I love my plants. I identify as Beesexual, they're all I need. But you knew that."

Cane frowned. "So you're asking for the cadet to live with you here? Also if you can't get out of here, how do you know about Commodore Kreeve and other things happening on base?"

James got up out of this chair and opened the door to his room. "They gave me a holovision that I don't think they realized is hooked up to the security cameras. So I have something fun to watch. Oh, and some rooms I get sound. Of course, this late at night there is nothing going on, just empty rooms. A few times you see a few of the officers getting busy. But that's about it."

Cane groaned, rubbing his temples. "They weren't supposed to put you on house arrest. The orders were to just keep an eye on you with only authorized visitors. I wanted you to be teaching a class. I'm going to have to talk to Admiral Ciccone about all of this."

"You said you were leaving, but Skyler said you were going to stay. Which is it? Because I don't get along with Davis."

Cane took a deep breath. "I'm staying but I really do have to go somewhere else for a little bit. While I'm away I will be gone for about two or three months, then I will be coming back. So after the exams. I have a few things to settle and then I will be off."

James narrowed his gaze. "Does it bother you Skyler turned out so much like his father?"

Cane frowned. "No, Skyler is very similar to his father but he is not him."

James looked at Cane's hands on his lap. "So you never did get married? Does it bother you Levi married the woman you wanted and had a son with her?"

Cane took a deep breath. "It used to until she rejected me around the time I became Fleet Admiral. I was there for part of Skyler's childhood. I never had my own children but as I see it Skyler is mine. I was there when he was born, almost married his mother, best friends with his father, was there for him as a child and now he is here in the forces. I get to finally be there for him all the time."

James nodded. "You sure you never had kids? Not even a bastard running around?"

Cane shook his head. "I was not that active and nobody has ever told me. I don't think it's possible. Skyler is my son and I will watch over him until the day he becomes a man."

The alarm went off. Dr. Fogg turned in his chair and looked at the red dot on the wall. "Anything personal you want to say, better say it now. That is Michael at the door."

Cane paused. "Naw, I think we're done here. I was just checking in."

Dr. Fogg stood up. "Well then, until we meet again." He opened the door and walked Cane to the door.

Before he opened it, Cane turned around and said, "I'm not making any promises but I will do my best to get you an assistant."

Dr. Fogg smiled. "I would love that, Lieutenant." He opened the door for Cane and Michael was on the other side.

Cane smiled at Michael. "Good day, Cadet Jones. Hope you enjoy your day."

Michael nodded. "I will, Cane."

Cane left the room.

Michael walked into the room and looked at Dr. Fogg, "What are we doing today?

Dr. Fogg smiled. "Prepping the plants we had in isolation for harvesting later today when Skyler and Perry arrive."

Chapter 16

Skyler put on his leather pants and dark green tank top. He combed his hair and put on his leather jacket.

Perry was putting on a pair of tight blue jeans. He looked over at Skyler. "Skyler, you know that this is a bar for old men. You're not going to get lucky."

Skyler turned away from the mirror and smiled. "I still got to look good. But not too good. If I was really serious I would dress sexier."

Perry raised a brow. "Sexier? You get half the girls here looking like that."

Skyler patted Perry on the back. "I could get half the women here dressed like you, and maybe a couple of guys," Skyler laughed.

Perry shook his head. "Twenty years from now, I still don't know if I will understand you."

Skyler laughed. "I don't know if I'm going to still want to hang out with you in twenty years."

He pouted and put on a red dress shirt. "So how are we getting there? It's in the city right?"

Skyler combed his hair one time, before he threw his comb on the bed. "I have convinced Kandy to give us a ride."

Perry's eyes widened. "And you're wearing that! Dude, you're bringing your girl to this club and you're dressed like you are trying to pick up women?"

Skyler shook his head. "I'm taking her as my friend. We're in an open relationship. I have no plans to pick up anyone. I just want to know why James keeps telling us to go."

Kandice knocked on the door and walked in. "Hey boys, your ride's here."

Skyler made his way towards the door. "Well then, let's get going."

They all walked into the bar. Skyler saw there were lots of young women who were about his age. He had never seen so many Catillions in one room before. He looked around and saw some older men sitting in the booths in the back of the room. He saw a few girls who got up to go talk to them.

Perry frowned. "Um, Skyler, aren't we supposed to go and sit in the back?"

Skyler shook his head. "We're not here to pick up anybody. Let's go sit at the bar."

They walked over the bar and grabbed three seats.

The bartender came over to them. "Ladies' night is Tuesday."

Skyler shook his head. "Two beers and a floral martini."

The bartender made them their drinks and came back. "Listen, since you boys aren't here for ladies' night I suggest you try table number four. Those guys are more your type."

Skyler kept a calm face. "Thanks, I will keep that in mind."

Perry's eyes were wide. "Did he just suggest we were here for the men?"

Kandice leaned over to Perry. "That's exactly what he meant. Hey, you're into cougars, maybe you could try a manther."

Perry shook his head. "No thank you. I got my hands full as it is."

Skyler turned around in the stool looking at the back walls and the men sitting at the tables. A sick feeling crossed his stomach. *Look at all these perverts, they're so old, find a girl your own age.* He turned back around and drank his beer. He got off his stool and walked over to this blonde with ringlets and a fluffy tail. "Don't you look lovely tonight."

The girl turned on her stool. "Where are your ears?"

Skyler laughed. "I'm human, not a Catillion, but I was wondering what a young lady like you is doing in a place like this?"

She reached out and touched Skyler's ears. "Humans have funny ears, they're not fuzzy. My name's Sherry by the way."

He smiled. "Skyler is my name. So you looking for a good time tonight?"

She shrugged. "I like older guys. They have experience and money."

Skyler grinned, "I got lots of experience and plenty of money. But I'm 21, do I count?"

She shook her head. "You're a boy. You need to get some grey and own a house first."

Skyler grinned, "I'm a cadet and I own a cabin back on Earth."

She giggled. "Sorry, you're just not my type, but maybe call me in 10-15 years."

Skyler nodded his head. "No problem, it was nice talking to you." He walked away making his way towards the bathroom. He stopped dead in his tracks when he looked ahead of him. He saw a guy getting up from the last booth. It was Commodore Kreeve. He was squeezed between two girls at the bar. Skyler hid from Kreeve and watched him go up to a dark red-haired cat. His mind filled with rage. He watched him flirt for a few moments; Kreeve was actually getting somewhere with this girl.

Skyler couldn't take it anymore and walked over to Kreeve with his fist clenched. "Miss, I would not do that if I were you."

She glared at Skyler. "And what business is it of yours?"

Kreeve glared at Skyler.

"Miss, this man raped a good friend of mine just a few days ago. He is a horrible man and uses women."

Kreeve looked at the girl and shook his head. He then turned to Skyler. "Just because you failed a test doesn't mean you have to tarnish my name, you little shit."

"I'm in none of your classes and I'm glad. I'm sick of your lies." Skyler took his fist and punched Kreeve in the face. "You jackass, I know what you did to Kax! And you came here looking for another girl. Get out of my face before I beat your ass!"

Kreeve rubbed his jaw and whacked Skyler square in the jaw, knocking him to the floor. He kicked Skyler while he was down.

Skyler grabbed his foot pulling him down to the ground. He sat on top of the guy and started punching him over and over. "You heartless bastard, you deserve to die!"

Security came and pulled Skyler off. The bouncers escorted both of them out of the building.

The biggest of the two bouncers said, "you two stay out or I will call the cops."

Skyler glared at Kreeve. He then saw from the corner of his eye Kandy and Perry walked out of the building. They came to Skyler's side.

"You have a lot of explaining to do, asshole!" Kandice said, "Kax is my sister!"

Perry made a fist. "You hurt Kax bad. She's my friend too!"

Kreeve brushed himself off. "She is my girlfriend, and is mine to do with as I please! If she wants to act like a whore then I will treat her like one!"

Skyler couldn't hold back. He punched him as hard as he could, knocking him to the ground and knocking out a tooth. Skyler kept beating on him. "You deserve to have your balls cut off you piece of shit!"

There was a loud siren and the cops showed up. They grabbed Skyler, dragging him off.

Skyler struggled to break free. "Don't arrest me, he's the bastard! He raped my friend!"

Kreeve got up and dusted himself off. "I called the cops the second I saw you. I knew you wouldn't let anything go."

Kandice made a fist. Perry grabbed her hand holding her back. He whispered into her ear, "Now is not the time, there are cops here."

Kandice spoke out. "Skyler is just mad because this creep raped my sister."

The cop raised his hands. "Okay, listen to me, we need to all take it easy and relax. You're all coming down to the station. We have two cars here, and you, miss, and your friend will have to drive down."

Once Skyler and Kreeve were in the cars, Kandice asked, "What's going to happen to Skyler?"

The cop shook his head. "I don't know, ma'am. We are going to put him in a holding cell until morning. We have to check his file."

Kandice nodded. "Thank you, officer. We will meet you down there."

Perry put his phone away when he was finished texting. "I sent Kax and Cane a message about Skyler. They're on their way."

***

When they got to the police station Kax and Cane were already waiting for them. Kax gave her sister a hug. "What happened? Perry just said Skyler was arrested?"

Kandice took a deep breath. "We went to this bar and he saw Kreeve trying to pick up another woman. Skyler saw and started beating him. Kreeve called the cops and well now we are here."

Cane rolled his eyes. "I wish he was on base when this happened then I would be able to deal with this quietly. I'm afraid since this happened on Catillion soil, Skyler, we will have to deal with Catillion laws."

Kax's eyes widened and she looked at Cane. "He did it to defend my honor, isn't there something you can do?"

Cane shook his head. "At this point I might. We just have to make sure that Kreeve doesn't press charges. Which might involve me cutting him a deal."

Tears began to run down Kax's face. "No, don't let Skyler suffer, and that bastard doesn't deserve any deal!"

Cane took a deep breath. "I will go in there and see what I can do. No promises, but I will do my best." He went up to one of the officers and they took him into a room.

Kax went and sat down. She cried into her hands. *Oh Skyler why, are you so stupid and do these things? We all don't need to lose our careers over this.*

***

Cane walked into the room with the police officer.

The man sat at his desk and looked at Cane. "So Leon Cane, what do you wish to talk to me about?"

Cane put his hands on his lap and spoke in a serious tone. "I'm here to defend Skyler Therris. He is my cadet and I want to make sure there is no mark on his record and—"

"I'm going to stop you right there. This boy committed a crime and has to be punished. Kreeve has already said he is pressing charges," the officer said.

Cane snickered. "Well, if that is so, then I want you to hand me the file and since they are both officers, I will deal with them on base."

The officer shook his head. "I can't do that, it was on Catillion soil. Your cadet is looking at two years in prison."

Cane shook his head. "Two years is too long, he can't do that. Why is it so long?"

"Assault and battery of a local and he is not from here. That's considered a hate crime."

"Listen, Kreeve already has charges of rape on him. The Catillion crying in the waiting room is the woman he raped. Skyler was just defending her honor, let him go!"

The cop shook his head. "That is a charge that has been placed on him on your base not on civilian land, two different matters. Now if you want Skyler back, there is a bail set for $2000. Are you willing to pay that?"

Cane's eyes bulged. "2000, why so high?"

The officer pulled up Skyler's file and showed his record. "He has quite a record and seems to be a troublemaker on Squall, and Kreeve is clean. If anything, from looking at this, I would think Skyler is the rapist."

Cane slammed his hand on the desk "SKYLER IS NOT A RAPIST!" He pulled out his wallet and dropped $2000 on the desk. "There is the bail. Just give me my cadet!"

The officer frowned. "Who carries that much money in their wallet?"

Cane glared. "That's none of your business."

The officer got up out of his seat and left the office. A few minutes later he returned to the office with Skyler in handcuffs.

A tear came to Cane's eye when he saw the bruises and scratches on Skyler's face. The officer let him out of the handcuffs. He handed Cane a tablet and said, "sign here and he will be free to go. We have Skyler's information and will let him know when the court date is set."

Cane signed the tablet.

The officer took the handcuffs off Skyler and let them out of the room.

Cane gave Skyler a hug. "You got to stay out of trouble. I'm just so worried about you okay? You're too reckless."

Skyler hugged Cane back. "I did it for Kax."

Cane frowned. "We will talk about this later. Right now let's go home and get rest. You have classes tomorrow."

Kax saw them in the hall and ran up to Skyler and gave him a hug. "Skyler, you stupid lovable idiot. Thank you, but never do that again!" She gave him a big kiss on the lips.

Skyler smiled and kissed her back. "I did it for you, don't you worry about me."

Kax didn't fight Skyler off. "Kandice and Perry are in the car waiting."

Skyler frowned, "In the same car? How did you get here anyway?"

"I gave Kax a ride." Cane said.

Skyler smiled. "I guess I will be riding with you on the way back?"

Cane nodded. "Yes, I think that would be best."

***

Kax went out to the car to check on Perry and her sister to let them know they could go home now. She walked out to the car and her eyes popped. "What the HELL!" She screamed. Kandice was in the back seat and she covered her breasts. Perry picked up his head from the back seat.

Kax went right to the car. "Perry, aren't you seeing someone? And Kandice, you're dating Skyler!"

Kandice got off Perry, and put her shirt on. "Skyler and me are open and plus I think we're about to break up any day now."

"Stellik and me aren't serious." Perry put on his pants. "Why can't I get a good girl for once?"

Kax frowned. "Perry, my sister is a whore. She's as far as you will get from good. Either way you can go back to the dorm and do whatever. Skyler is out and me and Cane are taking him back."

Kandice grinned at Perry. "Well, Perry, let's go home and have some fun."

Perry climbed back into the front seat. "You can tell Skyler about this and that I wish him well."

Kax waved goodbye to Perry and got into Cane's car. He went up to Skyler who was leaning on the hovering town car. "Perry fucked my sister. Just thought I would let you know, he said I could tell you, and he wishes you well." She walked around the car and got into the back seat.

Skyler was baffled. "What do you mean they fucked? When? Just now? I didn't think Perry had it in him."

Kax leaned out of the car. "Get in and I will tell you more. Where's Cane?" She closed the door.

Skyler got into the front passenger side. He looked back in the car. "Cane forgot something in the station and went back. But really, Perry and your sister? How does this make you feel?"

Kax frowned. "What do you mean make me feel? You're the one who should be upset."

Skyler shrugged. "Naw, she can fuck whoever she wants and so can I. We're just buddies. I'm glad Perry got lucky but he is not her type."

Cane got into the car. "Well I convinced them to hold onto Kreeve for the night but he will be walking around after that. I have him on suspension for now. Tomorrow, Skyler, I will see about moving your case to the base and not civil. If I get my way you will not see one day in prison."

Skyler shrugged. "Well, if I have to spend the summer there, I can do it."

Cane shook his head and began to drive. "No you're too high of a cadet now. If you don't do studies you are sent to work in the summer months. In a sense you belong to the Forces, and if you go to a civilian prison you will lose your career."

"You stupid idiot, Skyler! Why would you risk your career?" Kax called from the back seat.

Skyler turned and frowned at her. "I did it for you. We should all be lucky I didn't kill him. I wanted to rip his throat out or cut off his dick."

"I'm glad you didn't do that, but this is all getting out of hand." Cane said in an angry tone. "I just hope I can still get my month off. If nothing new is added to the list of charges I can have all these cases dealt with quickly. But if you make this worse then that makes my job harder. You kids all need to smarten up."

Kax leaned forward. "Cane, I'm sorry."

Cane sighed. "It's not your fault, you're the victim. I'm edgy because I'm on a deadline to get some stuff done on another planet and the drama here is building and I may never get back there."

Chapter 17

Skyler stepped out of the simulator. He took off his gas mask and wiped the sweat off his forehead. He peeled off the shell of the bean pod and took out a 2-inch bean and popped it into his mouth.

Dr. Fogg came up to him. "So how did the tests go?"

Skyler finished his bite of food. "Pretty good, I got all the bad guys quicker. It didn't take long to decontaminate and these beans taste better than the last."

Dr. Fogg took his clipboard and checked off a few things. "Good. Do you think this batch is the one?"

Skyler nodded. "I think it will be hard to top this one in efficiency."

Dr. Fogg patted Skyler on the back. "Well then you know what to do, captain. Fill out the survey and we will get testing on the next one."

Skyler took the clipboard survey and looked at Dr. Fogg. "You know I hate these surveys."

Dr. Fogg nodded his head. "That's called science paperwork. You would have more paperwork than that if you had an office or a government job. You got to document everything for the future to know."

Skyler frowned. "You know, I got arrested because of you."

Dr. Fogg frowned. "That's an odd change of subject but anyway, tell me what happened!"

Skyler sighed. "I went to the club like you said to and, well, I saw Commodore Kreeve there, trying to pick up another girl and I beat the crap out of him. He punched me too. That's how I got these marks on my face." He turned his head and showed the bruises on the side of his face.

Dr. Fogg looked at Skyler. "I got something for that, let me get it." He walked off to go to the plants. "I'm sorry this happened to you. I knew you would bump into him there, it's his favorite club. I didn't think it would get this bad. So what else happened?"

"He called the civilian cops, had me arrested and is pressing charges."

Dr. Fogg's eyes widened. "Shit, I'm sorry about that. I had no idea. You could get jail time. Is Cane going to help you out?"

Skyler walked over next to Fogg who was picking at some plants. "I'm looking at two years because of my past record. Cane is trying to get it moved to a base record so I don't lose my career. He also paid my bail."

Dr. Fogg picked a bright red cactus leaf off one of the plants and handed it to Skyler. "Cut it open and rub it on your face. It's like an aloe plant but much stronger."

Skyler used his thumbnail and sliced it open and rubbed the juices on the side of his face.

Dr. Fogg sighed. "Cane will get it changed. I mean he was able to keep me alive. Well he got me sent here forever, but it all worked out for the better in the end I suppose. But you do not want to be in a Catillion prison. They're very aggressive and territorial, you will be fighting to survive every day and the tough ones will like you because of your ears."

Skyler covered one of his ears. "Why my ears?"

"Same reason Kandy likes your ears, silly." Dr. Fogg laughed. "There might be a human gang now but back when I was there, there wasn't. When I was first transferred out here I had a horrible two weeks. Human prison is nicer, the guards don't want to get in on the action."

Skyler finished wiping his face. "You're kidding right? Please tell me you are. I have never been to prison, but I have been in some bad holding cells with people."

Dr. Fogg chuckled and took the empty leaf from Skyler. "Trust me, prison is nothing like the worst of holding cells. I have been in quite a few. In prison there will not be much protecting you from sharing a bunk with a big mafia cat."

Skyler got an uneasy feeling in his pants. "Ugh, I'm really not going to like this am I?"

James laughed. "If people liked it, it would not be a punishment. Don't worry, Cane will not let you spend one day in prison. He cares about you a lot. I have no idea why he ever liked me."

Skyler shrugged. "He likes people for the oddest reasons. I guess that's why he is a Fleet Admiral."

James laughed and patted Skyler on the back. "There is so much you don't know."

Michael and Perry entered the lab carrying two baskets of bean guns.

"We got your next batch ready to go," Perry said.

James smiled. "Perfect I will reset the simulator."

Chapter 18

Skyler opened the door for Kandice.

She entered the room and looked at him. She was wearing a tight blue tank top and tight blue jeans where her red thong was sticking out on the side. She kissed Skyler and said, "you ready for our date tonight?"

Skyler shook his head. "I'm sorry but no." He stared at her curvaceous body, the old feelings came flooding back, but he shook his head. "It has nothing to do with you and Perry. I just don't feel it's right to continue seeing you after what happened to your sister."

Kandice nodded. "I understand. I'm just shocked you're the one breaking up with me."

Skyler smirked. "I'm sorry but I don't think it's right. She has felt uncomfortable with our relationship since she found out. I really like you but we both knew it was temporary."

She leaned in and kissed Skyler. "It's okay. We don't have that much in common and I mostly stayed because of your sexy tongue. I wish there was a way to make a copy of it. Is there any chance we can still go out one last time?"

Kandice kissed Skyler. "Just one more time? What if I get a craving for your tongue and you're single?"

"I will give you three more times with me after tonight. Anytime you are near and want me, call me up. You can use them right away or wait a few years, this offer will not expire."

She played with his ears. "I think I can live with that."

A ringing came from Skyler's communicator. He broke away from Kandice and went to his bed and answered it. "Hello?"

"Skyler I need to go to the house tomorrow and I want you to help me out. Can you come with me and my sister?" Kax said on the other line.

Skyler turned to Kandice and said, "you came to see me the night before your taking your sister up to the house?"

Kandice pointed to the clock on the desk. "I was planning on seeing you first and taking her up tonight."

Skyler frowned. He moved the phone back to his ear. "Okay Kax, that sounds great. Your sister is here right now. I will just go up to the house with you tonight, sleep on the couch or something. If that is okay?"

"Sure. My dad's gone now so you won't have to worry about him pulling out his shotgun," Kax assured him.

Skyler let out a nervous laugh. "I'm sure glad about that. We will be by the room in a bit. Take your time getting ready. See you in a bit."

He hung up the phone and turned to Kandice, "Well I say we have about half an hour. Want to have some fun?"

Kandice leaned closer and kissed him passionately on the lips. "You bet we do."

***

Kax heard a knock at her door. "Skyler, Kandice, is that you?"

Skyler called back. "You bet, got your overnight bag packed?"

Kax opened the door with a pack on wearing her civilian clothes. "Yup, and we will be home in time for supper."

Skyler looked at the time on his tablet. "Supper is at 9 p.m. for you?"

Kax shrugged. "Not normally but I called Tom ahead and he said he would have Layla wait until we got there. They're excited to see you again. I told Layla you were coming and she was going to look up some human food for you."

Skyler frowned. "You live about 45mins away and you only found out that I was coming half an hour ago? How fast can she make human food?"

Kax shook her head. "I told her yesterday, I knew if I invited you to come to my house without my dad you would say yes."

"I have no choice but to agree with you there." Skyler smiled.

"Okay then, let's get going. We don't want to be late," Kandice said walking down the halls.

Once at the house, Kax walked in and saw Tom sitting on the couch. She ran up, jumped on the couch and hugged her brother. "Hey Tom, how are you doing?"

Tom tried to push his sister off him. "I'm good, but you're trying to crush me again."

Kax kissed her brother on the cheek and got up. "You're just a crybaby."

"I'm not, you're just a mean big sister!" Tom said pushing Kax back.

Kandice frowned. "Break it up, you two, or I will have to call daddy!"

Kax and Tom threw pillows at Kandice and stuck their tongues out.

Skyler laughed. "You guys are funny."

Layla came over and handed Skyler a beer. "They're always like this. It's a sibling thing."

Skyler took the beer. "I don't have siblings so I wouldn't know."

Layla smiled. "So sad, you don't know what you're missing. I come from a litter of four."

Skyler took a sip. "Four? Wow, that must be a lot to handle at once. Humans have problems with just having twins."

Kax got off the couch and walked over to Skyler and Layla. "One at a time is the dumb way humans do it. Because when you have a few at a time you can get it all done at once and not worry about doing it again and again."

Skyler smiled. "Kax, you want kids?"

"I would like to hopefully have some one day." Kax paused reflecting on the events the year before when she had the false pregnancy and found out she had Cantaltion. "I want them one day but only with my husband when we settle down and I have the time to focus on a family. I'm not raising kids with a boyfriend who can pack up and leave."

Skyler smiled. "You know my offer's always open. Also if your boyfriend or husband runs off on you, I will adopt the kids."

Kax let out a sigh remembering Skyler being by her side last year during the false pregnancy. "Like I said Skyler, it's not the time."

"I just wanted you to know where I stand." He took a sip of his beer.

Kax shook her head. "Thank you."

Tom heard from the couch. "Skyler, come sit on the couch and watch the game while Layla gets the food ready."

Skyler left Kax and went over and joined Tom on the couch.

***

"Well that was a lovely meal Layla. Thank you for the lasagna, it was wonderful. You're really are a good cook. Tom is lucky to have you."

She stood up to clear the table. "Thank you Skyler."

"Do you need any help in the kitchen?" Skyler offered.

"It's fine, Skyler, you are a guest. Me and Kax have got it, you and Tom go and relax." Layla said.

Tom wheeled away from the table. "Well Skyler since they're going to be busy cleaning the kitchen, want to come with me to and catch the rest of the game?"

"Sounds like a good idea to me." Skyler stood up and pushed in his chair. He walked around the table.

Tom looked at Skyler. "Hey I forgot something in my room. Can we go there?"

Skyler shrugged. "Sure, why not?" He followed Tom into his bedroom.

"Could you please close the door, since you're closer?" Tom asked Skyler.

"Sure." Skyler closed the door. "What's up?"

Tom turned around and looked at Skyler. "Not trying to pick on you. I think you're a great guy and Kax does like you but you have to be careful about what you say about her choices in men."

Skyler frowned. "What are you talking about?"

Tom took a deep breath. "She was molested in high school by a guy like you. The type of guy who was a jock, pretty boy had all the women he wanted. Kax was dating him in high school and he tricked her into losing her virginity and used her. She gave in to another guy who seemed nice for a change, but he did the same thing to her. She doesn't trust men. You seem like a nice guy and I don't think you would do that but I'm not her."

Skyler listened to the story. "Is this by any chance the same guy who she had car sex with?"

Tom thought about it. "I'm not sure but if she did that with anyone it would be him. He always drove her home while they were dating."

Skyler clenched his fists. "I hate guys like that. Does he still live in the city? I'll beat him up for her."

Tom frowned. "No one here has had contact with him since, and doing that would just piss Kax off." Tom gave Skyler an odd look. "Do you like to fight? Because if you're going to beat up all of Kax's jerk boyfriends you are going to have a long list."

Skyler scratched his head. "Oh, Kandy told you about Kreeve, didn't she?"

Tom nodded. "Oh yeah. I hope you get the charges dropped. He is an ass. I would defend her but, well, you know." He looked down at his chair.

Skyler nodded. "How many jerk exes does she have?"

Tom tried to think. "She doesn't tell me everything, but I would say at least five."

Skyler rubbed his face. "She needs to start picking up better men."

"Well, she did, like your friend Michael. She thought he was cute. Is he a good guy and single?"

Skyler's heart stopped. He had no clue Kax liked Michael. *What does he have that I don't?* "Yes, but Michael is more asexual, at least that's what he says. He is the kind of guy you trust your wife with. Meanwhile I'm the kind of guy you hire him to keep away."

Tom laughed. "And that's why I like you. You're so funny."

There was a knock at the door. Layla walked in. "Hey boys when you're done having alone time, come on out and join us in the living room."

Skyler smiled. "Ya I was just helping Tom with something. We will be out in a moment."

Tom wheeled back. "That's our cue to go."

Skyler made his way into the living room and sat on the couch next to Kax. Kax had a bowl of popcorn on her lap. He put one arm around her and reached in and grabbed some popcorn, "so what are we watching?"

Kax didn't move away from Skyler. "We are watching a movie about a Catillion who climbs a mountain and finds a missing city on the other side."

"Sounds good to me."

***

When the movie was over Skyler opened his eyes and stretched on the couch. "Movie over? How did it end?"

Kax pushed Skyler off her. "You fell asleep on me and it all went well. He chose to stay in the village and live with his new wife and family. Now it's time to go to bed."

Skyler sat up on the couch. "Ya where am I sleeping tonight?"

Kandice smiled. "Well you can sleep in my room, dad's room or the couch. Your choice."

Skyler rubbed his face. "Your dad's room seems a bit awkward for me tonight. The couch is very comfy."

"Those weren't really options." Kandice shook her head. "You're staying in my room and that's final. I want your company."

Skyler shrugged. "Well it doesn't look like I have a choice."

Kandice got up from her seat and took Skyler's hand, guiding him up the stairs.

Chapter 19

Skyler woke to a call of his name. He heard "Skyler, Skyler, time to wake up!" He got up out of bed and answered the door naked.

Kax quickly turned her face away from Skyler when she saw his nakedness. "Skyler, put on some pants before you answer the door please."

Skyler rubbed his face and turned around and put his shorts on. "You can look now, they're on. Sorry, my shorts are not something I think about."

Kax turned back around and watched Skyler get dressed. "So you had sex with my sister again after you broke up?"

Skyler pulled down his shirt. "No, we made out a bit but I was too tired. She didn't want me to wear shorts."

Kax rolled her eyes. "Well I hope you slept well because we have a busy day."

Skyler looked at the clock. "Well I'm late for work, if that helps."

Kax shook her head. "Cane gave you and me the day off, he sent me an email. My dad gave me the key to my mom's old storage locker and he wants the kids to clean it out. Cane told me that he was looking for a few things and so I said I would take you along and we could look in there first."

Skyler combed his hair in the mirror. "Sure, we can do that. Cane was looking through my dad's stuff a while ago too. I guess there are some things still missing."

Kax nodded. "Breakfast is ready so we can grab some bacon and eggs and then head out to the locker."

Skyler flowed Kax down the stairs. "Ya, this sounds like it will be fun."

***

Skyler got out of Kandice's hover-car that Kax borrowed. He followed Kax to the storage locker. The building was closed in like a giant metallic box. The unit numbers glowed in the dark. Inside all the sizes of the units were color-coordinated in a rainbow of colors.

"Hmmm, it must be around here somewhere. I thought he said it was one of the medium sized ones." She looked up and down the rows.

Skyler leaned over and looked at the number. Then he went ahead to look around. "Kax, I found it!" He said, calling from two rows over in the green row.

Kax's eyes widened. "That's huge. It's got to be one of the 20x20 units. I thought it was smaller. You could almost live in there."

Skyler laughed. "How many days is Cane willing to give us off?"

Kax opened the door to find out that the unit was only a quarter filled. She frowned, "Why after all these years would he be paying for a unit like this if all this stuff could fit into a smaller one? This has got to be about a thousand dollars a month or more." Skyler shrugged. "No idea but let's get these boxes sorted through as soon as we can. There is still a lot of stuff."

Kax leaned down and picked up a box. "I have no idea what is in any of these. No one has touched them since my mom died. Our job is to go through, find what we want, then I will let the others look. I talked to Tom and Kandice, they both agreed to let me look first."

Skyler watched Kax open up one of the boxes. "Does your dad know I'm with you here?"

She shook her head. "No, but it doesn't matter." She looked in the box and pulled out a tiny little onesie. "Aw this is our old baby clothes. Oh my gosh, I was that tiny once. Look Skyler." She held the light pink onesie up for Skyler to see.

He smiled. "It's hard to imagine you were that little. They're like doll clothes."

She put the outfit back into the box, "I will keep this box for Tom. He and Layla are going to need baby supplies sooner than me or Kandice."

Skyler nodded. "Ya Kandy got the implant so I don't think she is going to be having kids."

Kax's eyes widened as she reached for another box. "What? She got the implant, does she know what that does?"

Skyler frowned. "Don't they take it out when you want to have kids?"

Kax shook her head. "Yes but there is more to it than that. They place the implant inside you and it stops your reproduction system until you want to have kids. When you do decide to have kids, you have to take a course and prove you're married and fully committed. If you and your partner pass, you can try to have kids."

Skyler frowned. "That's what I thought. Sounds easy enough if you're serious."

Kax held up her finger. "That's the thing they're not safe. They have chemicals that can become toxic and if you don't get sick they will stay in your system and can cause birth defects. If a man is too big he can break it, causing irreparable damage. Or they rot your insides out preventing you from having kids. They aren't safe."

Skyler frowned. "Why do they promote them then? How do you know so much?"

Kax took a deep breath. "When I was in high school, they used to promote them to us as teens. I thought about it. It didn't matter if you were a virgin or not you could get one. I really was going to get one, until one of my friends in school got sick. I took her to the hospital and the nurse told me it was from her implant. My sister knows about this too. I wonder why she still did it?"

Skyler shrugged. "Don't look at me, I never told her to get it. I don't think she even plans on having kids if that makes you feel better."

Kax opened the next box. "I will have to talk to her about it. But thanks for telling me." She looked inside the box. "Aw, look Skyler, it's all my old baby toys. These are so sweet. I can't believe my mom kept them."

Skyler pulled out a pull-along cat toy with wheels. "Was this one Tom's?"

Kax nodded. "Ya he wanted a toy like him. When we were little my mom didn't make much money, she was just a Lieutenant. When she died, she was a commodore so my dad got a really nice pension. We didn't have the money to buy all the fancy toys so my dad improvised and did his best to find toys that looked like us."

Skyler spun the wheels of the toy before putting it back in the box. "Your dad seems like a very caring guy. I admire that even if he hates me."

Kax moved the box aside and grabbed another. "He will like you one day, he just is protective of us he has no one else. He never moved on, like your mother."

"Ya my mom moved on and I don't think she will ever like you." Skyler scoffed.

Kax opened the box and looked inside. There were a few books and a sealed wooden box. She picked up one of the journals. A nice green leather bound book. She opened it to the first written-on page. "March 2nd 148GA I miss my kids so much, space is lonely out here, Levi is by my side but the longer this mission continues the more distant he grows. I have gone by his room a few times and I swear I heard him crying. I wish there was some way he could see his son." She looked up and flipped a few pages. "I think these are her journals from when she was with your father."

Skyler grabbed one of the books and opened to a page at random, "February 11th 148GA. Last night Levi showed me the most wonderful time. I was sad that I had missed my kid's birthdays. Kax is getting so big. Levi planned a lovely candlelight dinner in his room made up of all our kids' favorite foods. He bought me a little cat plush toy so I won't be lonely. When dinner was done we sat and looked at pictures of our kids. Little Skyler looks so much like his father. Afterward he took me to his bed and we made sweet, sweet love. His hands were so gentle and caring as he caressed my-" Skyler closed the book. "I'm not reading any more of this."

Kax blushed. "Well it sounds like they really did love us."

"I never doubted that they didn't care." Skyler said remorseful.

She put the books back and pulled out the wooden sealed box.

Skyler looked at the box. "Looks like a small portable captain's chest." He took the box from Kax and looked at the bottom. "Her name is on the box. I wonder if my dad got it for her. These were only given to captains and first officers."

Kax looked in the cardboard box for the key. "Found the key. It was at the bottom of the box."

Skyler set the wooden box down. He took the key and turned it in and opened it up.

Kax's eyes popped. She quickly turned her head. "Oh dear no!"

Skyler laughed as he picked up the phallic like object. He pressed the on button and it began to vibrate. "Hey Kax, almost 20 years and it still works. Want to try it out?"

Kax covered her face. "Skyler, put that away."

He turned it off, put it back in the box and could not contain his laughter. He picked up the actual phallic object and examined it. "I get it Kax you don't like things that vibe you just want to use a nice dong like this." He jokingly shook the toy around in Kax's face.

With a beet red face she grabbed it from him. She looked at the thing in her hand, "Why does it say LT on the bottom? Lieutenant?"

Skyler raised an eyebrow. "Levi Therris?"

Kax dropped the toy back into the box. Horrified she asked, "is that your dad's dick?"

Skyler picked it up. "I think it's a copy, a good copy." He looked at it. "Thanks dad for the good genes."

Kax grabbed it from Skyler and threw it in the box, closing it and quickly putting it away. "No, we are not talking about this again!"

Skyler grabbed the box. "This is history and that's a copy of my dad's dick."

Kax frowned. "Skyler, what are you going to with a copy of your dad's dick? Give it to your mother? You really want to keep it? You can have it if you want."

Skyler thought about it for a moment. "Ya I guess we can throw them out but keep the box, it's rare."

She put the box back in the cardboard box. "We will just put it aside for now, let's look at the other stuff."

Kax grabbed another box and opened it. She looked inside, "Oh look, Skyler, it's my mom's old cadet uniform."

Skyler looked at the tag. "She's the same size as you. You should try it on. These old uniforms were cool. They had longer skirts and sleeves."

Kax pulled it out of the box and examined it. "Ya they shortened the skirt because these long ones got caught on things too easy. But the gold trim was nice. I guess I could try it on." She looked at Skyler. "How do you know my size?"

Skyler smiled. "I have read your tag a few times just to know in case I ever need to buy you clothes."

She frowned at Skyler. "Never buy me the clothes you're thinking of." She looked around the room. "There is no real place to change. I will try it on at home, but keep it for now."

Skyler looked closer at it as she put it in the box. "It still has the pilot division pin on it. She must have forgotten to turn that in, or someone let her keep it. If you don't want it you can always sell it, some collector will want it."

"I will keep it," said Kax. "I'm the pilot in the family. I'm sure no one will object to me having it. I'll try it on at home though." She grabbed another box, "Come on Skyler, we got lots to go through."

***

Night time came and Skyler drove them back as Kax slept in the passenger seat. He pulled up to the driveway. He parked the car and put his hand on Kax's shoulder. "Time you wake up we're home."

She opened her eyes and rubbed her face. "Thank you Skyler, you're so sweet."

He smiled. "Come on, we can unload the car tomorrow. You worked hard going through that many boxes."

Kax unbuckled her seat belt and followed Skyler into the house.

The house was dark and there was a note left by the door. 'Gone to bed early. Food is in the fridge -Layla'

Skyler's tummy began to rumble. "Hey Kax you want some food or do you want to go to bed?" He looked at Kax who had fallen asleep on the couch. He smiled. "I guess I will sleep in her room tonight then."

He looked at the food in the fridge: mashed potatoes and meatloaf. He grabbed one of the plates and enjoyed his food. Once he was done he put the plate in the sink and washed it off.

He went up the stairs and debated if he should go to Kax's room or David's. *Damn my morals.* He went over to David's room and slept there for the night.

Chapter 20

Morning came. Skyler was woken to Kandice pouncing on the bed and sitting against his morning wood. He tried to move but she pinned him down.

She kissed his lips. "Morning, hot stuff."

Skyler awkwardly smiled. "We broke up remember?"

She rubbed her hands down his chest. "I like you too much to let you go. Please can we do it again?"

Skyler half awake and gathering his thoughts he said, "Why don't I just give you a copy of my dad's dick? It's almost the same as mine."

She got off him. "Why do you have a copy of your dad's dick? Isn't he dead?"

Skyler laughed, "We found it in your mom's stuff, along with her vibrator, they're still both in good condition."

"Are you serious?" She gave him a crinkled look.

He nodded. "Your choice, I don't really want to throw it out but I have no idea what to do with it."

She kissed Skyler on the cheek. "I will think about it. Come on, time for breakfast."

Skyler got out of bed and put on his shirt. "What's for breakfast?"

She looked at him oddly. "Sausage and eggs. You slept in your pants? That's a first."

Skyler nodded. "It's your dad's room didn't think it was right to sleep in my shorts or less."

She shook her head. "You're silly he wouldn't know. But come on let's get some food."

Skyler made his way downstairs. He looked around and didn't see Kax. "Hey where is Kax?"

Layla put his plate down on the table. "She is in her room. She wanted to try something on or something."

"Oh I know what's she's talking about. I will be right back." He made his way up to her room and knocked on the door. "Hey Kax need any help with the uniform?"

"Yes they put this zipper in the back and it seems to be stuck." She called out.

He entered the room and zipped up the back of her jacket.

She turned around to show off the uniform. A long sleeved purple mandarin jacket with gold piping on the front flap, and a below the knee skirt in matching color with a slit on the side. She did a little twirl to show Skyler. "What do you think?"

Skyler smiled. "You look just wonderful, like a sexy flight attendant."

She blushed. "Skyler you're too kind."

He put his hand on her shoulder, leaned in and kissed her on the lips. "You are the most beautiful I have seen you yet."

She blushed and turned her face away. "Skyler, you're so sweet." She kissed him back. "Thank you for being so wonderful. Now help me get out of this."

He grinned, "I would love to get you out of that uniform."

She frowned at him. "Not like that, I just mean unzip me."

"Give me a moment, I want to get a photo of you. I don't think you will be wearing this again for a while." He went to Kandice's room and grabbed his tablet off her nightstand. He went back to Kax's room. "Make a cute pose for me."

She put one hand on her hip and blew a kiss with the other.

"Perfect." He took the picture. "One more pose."

She kept her hand on her hip and saluted this time.

He took the picture. "Looks great, I love it." He walked behind her and unzipped her uniform. "There you go. I will leave the room now, see you at breakfast." She turned around with her jacket still on. "Hey Skyler, thank you for everything."

He turned around and smiled. "What are friends for?"

Chapter 21

Skyler was on his way to the greenhouse when his communicator started to beep. He answered it. "Captain Therris speaking."

"What have I told you about saying that on the phone? You are not a captain yet." Cane said in an annoyed tone.

Skyler laughed it off. "Cane sorry I didn't realize it was you, it's just a nickname." He could hear Cane sigh.

"The day you become a Captain I will gladly call you that as much as you want but until then, stop it! Now get to my office, there is a lot we need to talk about."

He was just at the doorway of the greenhouse. "Yes sir I'm on my way now."

He made his way to the main hall up the stairs to Cane's office. He knocked on the door, "Cane it's Skyler."

Cane opened the door. "Get in we need to talk."

Skyler sat down at his seat in the corner. "What's up, you don't seem in a happy mood today."

Cane rubbed his head. "I have been up most of the night because of you. But first of all you can't answer your phone as Captain Therris, you're not a captain yet. Just say hello when you get a call. What you are doing is impersonating an officer. I know you do it in a joking manner but your voice is too similar to your father's and it bothers me."

Skyler rubbed his neck. "Sorry Cane, I will stop doing that. I didn't realize it bothered you so much. So what did you want to see me about?"

Cane took a deep breath. "Did you find anything on my list in Karmantha's stuff?"

Skyler frowned. "Who?" He paused and thought about it. "Oh Kax's mom, that's her full name. I forgot. No we didn't find anything but there are still more boxes. We found her old cadet uniform and her journals about her and my dad, and well their…toys."

Cane raised an eyebrow. "Toys?" He paused. "Oh those. I remember hearing about them. Can I see the journals? There might be a clue in one of them."

Skyler nodded. "They're in Kax's room. We figured you would want to see them. But we mostly found her old clothes."

"I'll leave a message for Kax to bring them when she can to my office." He flipped through a few pages on his desk and handed Skyler a folder. "I can get the trial moved here which is good, but if I do, Davis will be your judge. You might have a better case fighting in civilian court. If we were on Earth I would say ask your step-father for a favor but we're not—"

"If this case was on Earth and I asked Charles he would have me on trial for attempted murder and I would be there for twenty years. My uncle is the only one who likes me."

Cane rubbed his chin. "Okay well in that case, we have three options. We fight this in civilian court and get an acquittal, fight it here and let Davis deal with you, or easiest we have Kreeve drop the charges."

Skyler frowned. "Wait, if he drops the charges, then I'm free to go? I have money, my uncle has money, we can write him a check."

Cane sighed. "It is not that simple. Only if we stay in civilian court do we need to get him to drop the charges, if we move it here we can't back out."

"I have a decent record but I can justify losing my career over this, I did what I believe was right. I will just have to find something else to do. I guess I'm too wild and crazy for the job."

Cane shook his head. "No, you will not spend one day in prison as long as I'm breathing. Now here is the deal. I was ready to kick Kreeve out of the forces but if you want to settle out of court I might have to give him his job back. Are you okay with that?"

Skyler thought about it for a moment. "Will it be the exact same job or will it be different? Like can you send him to laundry duty on an ice planet or something?"

"Well it depends on what it takes to drop the charges. He won't be going back to being a deep space instructor, I will keep him away from the academy, but that won't be decided until the court date. But really it is how far are you willing to let this go?"

Skyler thought about it. "Whatever it takes. Kreeve's trial will do the most damage to him and his career so I'm not so worried. Try and bribe him first. I have tons of money."

"What if he wants you to buy him a moon?"

"As long as it's an ice moon."

***

Cane sat in the office reading one of Karmantha's journals when there was a knock at his door. He put the book down. "Come in," He called out.

Kreeve came to the door. "Fleet Admiral Cane, you wanted to see me."

He put the book into his drawer. "I want to talk about one of your upcoming court cases."

Kreeve stayed calm and sat down. "Which one?"

Cane pulled out a copy of his file and handed it to Kreeve. "This is your past military and police record, it is quite large. But this is not your first sexual assault case nor domestic violence. I wish to offer you a deal if you are willing to drop the charges on Cadet Therris and admit you are guilty to raping Cadet Tillion."

Kreeve frowned. "That little punk hit me first and knocked out one of my teeth and you want me to get let him run free?"

Cane pulled out his checkbook. "We are willing to pay your dental bill and then some, name your price."

"One million dollars." Kreeve stared him down.

Cane put his pen down. "Be serious about this. What do you want? Name your price, career or otherwise."

"Promote me to admiral and then retire me with a full pension. I have the hours and honors, you can give me the promotion."

Cane checked the computer. "You do have it all there. I could do that and I could say you were mentally unfit for duty. You still have to show up in court for Kax's trial and that I'm not in control of. That can be done. Anything else?"

"I still want that little brat to pay for my dental bills."

Cane nodded. "I can't do that. Just drop all charges and walk away with your promotion. You're still looking at jail time for what you did to Cadet Tillion, you do know that, right?"

Kreeve stared at him with dark eyes. "That bitch deserved it for cheating on me with that little prick."

Cane glared. "Oh ya, keep that attitude up, it will go over so well in court."

Kreeve got up out of his seat. "Trust me I taught her a lesson that she will never forget."

"Keep saying things like that and I will knock out your other tooth. I want your uniform and your kit turned in by noon tomorrow, you hear me!?"

Kreeve nodded. "You are such a hardass, Leon."

Chapter 22

Michael came over to the table and put his lunch tray down. "Well this is nice to all have lunch together again. It has been a long time."

Kax looked up from her plate. "You bet it is. Why do you three boys have lunch off anyway?"

"Parole hearing for James. Cane is trying to get his sentence adjusted."

Perry frowned. "Ya I don't know why Cane is so nice to him. He is a criminal."

Skyler frowned. "You have seen his skills, he is incredibly smart. I think that is part of the reason. He can do more than the basic human so I think he is too good to kill."

Perry frowned. "And the people he killed weren't?"

Michael sighed. "Perry, we are sorry about your uncle and his family but just be happy you are alive and you did not die."

Perry took a bite of his sandwich. "I guess you're right." There was a vibration coming from Perry's pocket.

Michael moved away from him. "What is that?"

Perry pulled out his communicator. "It was set to vibrate, sorry if it bothered you."

Michael shrugged. "It was not that bad."

Perry answered the phone. "Hello Perry Zyrix speaking." He listened for a moment. "Okay give me a second."

He put his phone down on the table and turned on the hologram feature.

Cane's face appeared. "Perry I'm in court right now with Dr. James Fogg and he has made a request of you. I would like to know your answer."

Perry took a sip of his drink. "Okay then, I'll listen."

The judge's face came on the hologram. "Cadet Zyrix, Dr. James Fogg is requesting for a partner like assistant to work with his plants and run errands for him because he can't leave the building. Your job would be to go wherever he sent you and stay with him in his greenhouse. Would you be willing to do this?"

Perry frowned. "For how long?"

"For as long as you wanted. Dr. James Fogg will never be allowed out of the greenhouse so this is a permanent full time position. You would be a working cadet, until you graduated. What do you say to that?"

Perry's heart stopped, he hated this man but he loved the plants. *Could I really live with Dr. Fogg?* He looked at Michael. "What about Michael? He likes the guy."

The judge said, "we already discussed Cadet Jones but he is needed elsewhere."

Kax smiled at Perry. "Do it. You love the plants and love to learn. Go on and take the job."

Perry took a deep breath. "This goes against all my feelings towards Dr. Fogg. But I would be willing to give it a shot."

The judge nodded. "Thank your Cadet Zyrix. That is all for now." The communication was cut.

Perry looked around the table at everyone. "Did I do the right thing?"

Skyler grinned. "I think you did. If there is anyone in the world who loves to watch grass grow it's you. You have a job and permanent posting. That is something we all wish for once we graduate."

Michael nodded. "He is right. I like working with the guy but plants are not my thing."

Perry put his head down on the table. "This isn't right. I hate the guy."

Kax reached out and put her hand on Perry's shoulder. "Perry you hate his actions but you clearly don't hate him or you would not have gotten this far in your work with him. I think it is good. Talk to your dad when he comes."

Michael frowned. "Was your dad not supposed to arrive a month ago?"

Perry picked his head up. "Yes he was but he had a few problems with the Earth borders. They have closed a lot due to the war so it is hard to get a flight out of there. So he is staying there for now in the hotel until he can get a flight here. He is thinking of getting one to Squall to visit my sister."

Kax took a deep breath. "I hope he is going to be okay. Why didn't he take the route passed Modoralean?"

"If it was going to be this bad he would have, when he left the colony it was safe to travel. But now it isn't. He can't even get back home."

"That must be really scary for him," Skyler said.

"No, he's lived through worse. He was a civilian during the last two wars. He knows what to do. He just has to wait a bit more is all."

"Well they didn't say that this was forever. You could see how it goes and if you really can't stand living with the guy then leave. They should give you a choice," Skyler said.

"You probably will not be there that often," Michael added. "He always talks about how there are plants from planets he cannot go to and wants to get their seeds. You will probably be traveling most of the time."

Perry sighed, picking at his food, "I'll talk to my dad. He will know what to do."

***

Perry sat at his computer desk waiting for the call from his dad. He sat there wondering what his dad might say. Skyler was out of the room for a night at the bar. He wished he could have gone with him too. Anything to get his mind off living with Dr. Fogg. It was something he was not looking forward to.

He stared at the screen waiting for the call. He got a dark feeling that something was wrong. He pulled up the news pages and looked to see if there was anything on an attack. To his horror his fear was right. There was another attack on Earth. *Please, please do not let him be dead or injured.*

A tear came to his eye. *Please don't let my father be dead.* He could not hold the tears back anymore, and his eyes filled with tears. There was a sharp pain in his chest, imagining what it would be like if his father was dead.

Then there was a bright light pop up on the screen. He looked up and answered the call.

"Hello there, son!"

Perry wiped the tears from his eyes. "Dad, you're alive!"

His father smiled. "Of course I am. Why would you think I was dead?"

"There was another attack on Earth and when you didn't call me on time I thought you were dead."

His father turned to the side. "I told you your clock was minutes too slow. Look what you did to poor Perry."

Perry frowned. "Who are you talking to, Dad?"

A cute blonde-haired girl with brown eyes and pigtails appearing onscreen. "Hey bro!"

Perry smiled. "Hey sis, what are you doing on Earth?"

She laughed. "We're on Squall. This is my dorm room." She picked up the laptop and moved it around the room. "See my dorm!"

Perry smiled. "So Dad, you made it to Squall, that's awesome!"

His father nodded. "Yup after I talked to you yesterday and sent you the message of when to talk to me next, I got a call saying that I could get a shuttle to Squall. I took it. I didn't have time to contact you and figured I would surprise you tonight. Guess I was lucky about the attack."

Perry nodded. "Well this was a great surprise. I love it, thank you Dad. It is nice to see you too, sis. How is Squall?"

She smiled. "I love it here. All the Squallite guys are so cute! Also they're so tall! I love it!"

Perry laughed. "You're 5'3. everyone is taller than you. But that's awesome. I'm glad you're happy. I have not been to Squall but my friends have been."

"Perry you would love it here, there's so much nature and wildlife. I want to stay here forever."

"Sis, it is your first planet you have been to, keep looking around. You will find others you love."

She smiled. "So how are you enjoying Catillion? Is it nice?"

"It's nice here. I like it. Very dark but I'm getting used to it. Been inside working in the greenhouse most of the time. I'm cutting back my classes next semester."

His father came back on. "Why are you cutting your classes back? Is there a problem?"

Perry shook his head. "No I will be working. I have been offered a job and right now I have agreed to take it."

His dad's eyes lit up. "You haven't even graduated and you have been offered a job? Good for you, son. What is it?"

Perry took a deep breath. "Well that's what I wanted to talk to you about dad. I have been given a live-in apprenticeship in the greenhouse. I will be growing plants and traveling to go out and get more plants."

"Perry, this is great! Good for you. It's what you always wanted right?"

Perry nodded. "Well I always wanted to do this kind of job on the colony, but I don't think I will be able to do that for a long time now."

"Perry you're still young, do this for years and when you are ready to settle down then you can apply for a transfer. Now what seems to be the problem you're not telling me?"

Perry looked down at his desk and sighed. "It's who I will be working and living with, Dad, that's the problem." He paused and took a deep breath. "I will be Dr. James Fogg's apprentice."

His dad's eyes widened. "The same Dr. James Fogg who killed your uncle's family? And all of Colony J!"

With a deep sigh Perry answered, "Same guy. He has admitted it to me and told me the story. He doesn't hide his past. But dad this is an opportunity of a lifetime. I know you don't like the man but I can work for him gain the knowledge and leave."

His father frowned. "Why? He is a mass murderer. Why would you work with him?"

"Because he is one of the most brilliant minds that has ever been born. I'm not a killer like him but if I can learn even half his knowledge I will go far in the world. I want to take this job and listen to everything he says."

"Who cares? This man killed your uncle, my brother!" His father snapped.

Perry nodded. "Yes he did and I know but he is also very smart and knows things no one else knows. I would like to work with him."

His dad sighed. "Don't make any choices yet. I will be out there by the end of the year, so right about the time your exams will be done. It will be interesting to meet this Dr. Fogg. I have never met him in person."

Perry nodded. "I can't wait to see you, Dad."

The door behind Perry opened and Skyler was sucking the face of some girl.

"Perry, is that your roommate from Earth? Sky something?"

Skyler pulled himself off the girl. "Hey Perry's Dad. You're right, it is me, Skyler. How are you doing?"

"Very good. I made it to Squall."

He took off his jacket. "Great to hear. I hope to see you soon. I would love to talk but I'm kind of busy."

The girl pulled Skyler onto the bed.

"Um, Dad, I'm going to let you and sis go. It is going to get a little noisy in here for a bit."

His dad laughed. "Sounds good to me, son. Have a good night."

His sister came on. "Night bro, talk to you later!"

He waved to both of them. The moaning in the background began. "Talk to you two later. I got to go."

The girl screamed. "Oh Skyler!"

"Got-to-go-bye!" Perry quickly turned off the computer screen. He got up from the desk and looked at Skyler. "You could have given me a few moments to say goodbye to my father at least."

Skyler and the girl were both naked now. He looked at Perry. "Sorry buddy but when a girl wants you, you can't make her wait. You could join in if you want?"

Perry grabbed his laptop and a textbook. "I'm going out to study."

Skyler had his face between the girl's large breasts now and was not able to respond.

Perry took his stuff and made his way out to the hall. He decided the only place for him to go was back to Stellik. He could have stayed in the room but he wanted to have some time to collect his thoughts and talk to someone who would understand. He walked through the courtyard to the commodore barracks. He knocked on the oval door.

A tall aging Squallite answered the door. "Perry, what are you doing here this late?"

He sighed, "I had a long day and I needed a break from the rest of the world, can I spend some time with you?"

She smiled. "Sure, you can come in. There's room for you."

He sat down on the couch, and put his laptop and books down on the coffee table.

"I was just about to make some tea do you want some?"

He nodded. "That would be great thank you."

"So what's new in your life? I haven't seen you for almost two weeks, I was wondering what you have been up to."

He rubbed his head. "I have been offered the job of Dr. Fogg's permanent apprentice."

Her eyes widened. "I didn't know he was taking an apprentice." She brought him a cup of tea.

Perry took the cup of tea. "I didn't know he was either. But he was in his parole hearing and I got a call asking if I would be willing to do this."

"Well I hope you said yes." She sat down next to him on the couch.

Perry blew on his tea and before taking a sip. "Well it is looking like I have no choice, everyone tells me how great of an opportunity this is but he is a killer."

She nodded. "Dr. Fogg is a very smart man. This is an opportunity of a lifetime. This is a great career move for you. I understand what you are doing is bothering you but you can do it."

He smiled. "Yeah and he's not too bad of a guy. I have been working with him most of this semester and he hasn't hurt anyone yet, if anything he has helped us all out."

"I have read his file and he is not violent unless you kill one of his plants so I think you should be fine." She took a sip of her tea.

He looked back at her. "Well maybe it is a good idea."

She leaned over and kissed him on the cheek. "You are a great guy, you know what's right."

He blushed. "I'm too young for you."

She placed her hand on his knee. "I know but I think you're cute. There is nothing wrong with a fling. Or someplace for you to go and rest your head when life gets too rough."

He shifted as his pants became tighter. "You got a point there."

She put her cup of tea down on the coffee table and kissed Perry on the lips. "Come on, let me release some of that tension for you."

He awkwardly smiled, putting his teacup on the table. "I guess that would be fine."

Chapter 23

Skyler knocked on Kax's door.

She called out. "Who is it?"

Skyler called back. "It's Skyler, can I come in and talk?"

"Just one second," she called out. A moment later she opened the door and tossed her hair back.

He smiled at her and walked in the door.

"Sorry about that Skyler. I was just finishing getting dressed." She looked at the clock and saw it was 5 a.m. "Wow you're up early?"

Skyler nodded. "Last time we have to test the weapons before the final growth cycle. It looks like these are really going to happen."

She smiled. "Well I wish you luck. I hope you have a good time in the simulator." She brushed her hair. "Did you hear about the attack on Earth?"

He sat down on her bed. "I did, and well, I'm glad we aren't there. Half the city got burnt."

"It was not just our city that got burnt. There were other countries that got hit too. This was our biggest attack yet."

"And my stepfather still couldn't get hit." Skyler scoffed.

She sat down next to Skyler. "I know how much and why you hate him but still do you really want him dead?"

Skyler nodded. "He wants me dead. He has told me that and even threatened to end my life. So, if I died in an attack he would be singing and partying."

Kax gave Skyler a hug. "I'm sorry to hear that. Really I am."

He shrugged. "It's no big deal. How is the new flight instructor?"

Kax took a deep breath and fell back onto the bed. "I hate her. She must have been trained by Davis. She is such a bitch. You think she would be thankful I was the reason she got the job, but no, she hates me and has told me that."

Skyler laughed. "She's not his wife is she?"

Kax's eyes widened. "He doesn't have a wife, he has an ex-wife. Oh no, what if that's her?"

Skyler tried not to laugh.

"Oh, Skyler, my whole life I have wanted to be a pilot in deep space and now I'm in training and I screwed it up. I didn't plan to date Kreeve, he just understood my love for piloting and I thought he was a kindred spirit." She rolled onto her stomach and buried her face in the blankets.

Skyler patted her on the back. "Could you apply for a transfer? I know this is for a year but there has got to be another port for you to do this training."

She looked up. "There is but it is on Capriac. I don't want to go there, it's too far away from anything. This is the best place for me to go."

Skyler looked at his tablet. "What is your flight instructor's name?"

She covered her face "Commodore Helga Adams, the meanest bitch in the fleet."

"Hey don't make my mother sound nice." He typed in her name and looked up her file. "Oh shit you are not going to like this."

She groaned. "Do I dare to ask?"

Skyler read the screen. "She is his ex-wife and they divorced because she caught him with a female student. So he has a record of being with cadets. I guess she sees you as a thorn in her side."

She covered her face. "Oh no, this is just terrible, I hate this. Skyler, make it stop."

Skyler shrugged. "Well you could talk to Cane. She is temporary, maybe he could find another person to take her place. The teachers aren't allowed to have any bias with the students. Kreeve didn't give you any extra points. You knew your stuff so she shouldn't knock things down."

Kax nodded. "Ya I think you're right, I will go talk to Cane, and also see about getting more time off. You and me need to finish looking at my mom's stuff."

Skyler frowned. "Why do I need to go back to the locker? You have the list."

"Skyler, I thought you enjoyed working in the locker with me?"

Skyler nodded. "I did, and would like to do it again, just things are getting so busy. I'm sorry but things are getting crazy and out of hand with exams. I wouldn't mind a few regular days off."

"Skyler, we got to get this done. I need your help, okay? We got two weeks off once exams come up. That should be enough time. One more month? I can see about Cane giving us a few more days at the locker."

Skyler sighed. "I don't know if I can. The plants are almost done."

"Skyler, let's go talk to Cane and figure out both these issues." She got up off the bed and headed for the door.

Skyler shrugged. "Well, I guess we can. I'll just explain to Dr. Fogg I'm running late."

They walked down the hall together and made their way to the main hall. Skyler knocked on Cane's door. "Cane are you in there? It's Skyler and Kax."

An unfamiliar face came to the door. "Hello cadets, are you looking for Fleet Admiral Cane?"

Skyler nodded. "Yes sir. Who, might I ask, are you and what are you doing in Cane's office?"

"I am Admiral Greenwood and Cane has been moved to the north side of this building to a more permanent location. Who are you two?"

Skyler smiled. "I'm Cadet Therris and this is Cadet Tillion."

Admiral Greenwood nodded. "Good he will be wanting to see you two. You better make your way."

Skyler and Kax both nodded and turned around and made their way to the north building. Looking for Cane's new office, they made their way down foreign hallways and trying the map Skyler had pulled up on his tablet.

Kax was about to ask someone for directions when Skyler turned a doorknob. "This way, found the room."

He walked into the room and looked around at the red velvet and up at the hardwood desk where a blonde Catillion secretary was sitting.

She looked up from her desk. "Hello can I help you two?"

Skyler nodded. "Ya, we are here to see Cane and we were told his office moved here."

She typed a few things into her computer. "Yes this is Fleet Admiral Cane's office but do you two have an appointment?"

Skyler rolled his eyes. "I'm Skyler Therris. I don't need an appointment."

She frowned. "I don't know what that means, but you need an appointment to see the Fleet Admiral. He is a very busy man."

"I'm tired of his secretaries not knowing who I am." He rubbed his forehead. "Just page Cane and tell him Skyler and Kax want to talk to him. If he says he is busy we will leave."

The secretary conceded and hit the intercom button. "Fleet Admiral Cane, there is a Skyler Therris and a Kax here to see you and they don't have an appointment."

Cane's voice was heard over the intercom. "Skyler doesn't need an appointment, let him in. I have a few minutes."

The secretary looked up at Skyler. "I guess you were right." She hit the button and opened the door.

They entered the room. Cane was unpacking a few boxes. "Sorry about the office change. I was just moved last night. Did you kids have problems finding it?"

They shook their heads. "No sir. But there are two reasons me and Kax are here to see you."

Cane peered up from the boxes. He sat in his chair. "I'm all ears. What seems to be the issue?"

Kax spoke up. "Cane, I have wanted to be a deep space pilot my entire life and, well, this year I kinda screwed that up royally. I know I am in no position to complain. But Commodore Adams is horrible and I can't stand her. She is constantly picking on me because she is Kreeve's ex wife. I know everything I need to know in this class. Is there a way I can just skip forward to the exams?"

Cane rubbed his head. "Well I am not really in charge of the flight area but I could see what I can do. I can see why she wouldn't care for you. When looking into things, I learned her husband has a thing for pilots. That's how they met."

Skyler rubbed his chin. "Wait if this guy has such a bad record why does he still have his job? Why has he been able to get away with it all these years?"

Cane pinched the bridge of his nose. "We don't keep track of everyone's sex lives here. But what I'm guessing is he has mainly gone for young pilots but not his students. That and others have not come forward. I'm trying to build a bigger case on him. As for Admiral Adams, I will see if we can get a better replacement. Until then if you don't wish to attend class I will write you a letter."

"Thank you but what about my final marks?" Kax asked.

Cane typed in a few things on his computer. "When I talk to the department I will let you know what they say. Worst case, they will make you do a make up test."

Skyler raised his finger. "Speaking of taking time off. We were going to ask when you would like us to go back to the storage unit?"

Cane smiled. "This is a perfect time. What if I excuse you two from classes for the week to send on this assignment?"

Kax smiled. "I wouldn't mind."

Skyler shook his head. "I love to miss class as much as the next person but we are getting really close to finalizing the plants. I don't know if I can leave for an entire week."

Cane paused for a moment in thought. "I will talk to Dr. Fogg, both these things are important but mine has a tighter time constraint. You kids have this one week to find the items I put on that list. I'm going to be leaving for the month and I need those items."

Kax tilted her head. "May I ask why these items are important?"

Cane took a deep breath. "I'm sure by now Skyler has shared with you some of his Father's things. Well, Levi died with a lot of unfinished business and I as his first officer and a witness to these events have a list of things to complete for him over time. Levi's death wasn't planned or expected so it makes sense that his stuff isn't in the right spots. I tried to get some things from Sandy but she denied me access or told me things had been destroyed and David never wanted to talk to me. He gave a lot of things to your mother Karmantha when he realized Sandy wasn't as trustworthy as he had once thought. He also loved and trusted her, he would have given her anything if she asked."

"Did my dad love Kax's mom more than my mother?" Skyler asked.

Cane let out a long sigh. "These things are so complicated. My feelings for your mother were different than Levi's feelings for her but we both loved her in different ways. When it comes to Levi and Karmantha, they were more compatible. If Levi would have met Karma first, history would've been much different."

They all sat in silence.

Skyler broke the silence. "We won't let you down Leon."

Cane smiled. "I know you won't. Now your two holidays start now, get working."

Chapter 24

"So, make a decision yet?" Dr. Fogg's voice said behind Perry. Perry's body tensed while he clipped a leaf off the plant. His hand was shaking, almost dropping the clippers.

"I'll take that as a no. Listen, Perry, before you hurt one of my plants, can we talk in my office?"

Perry let out a sigh and put down his pair of clippers next to the plant. He followed James into his office at the back of the greenhouse. Perry sat down in the chair in front of the desk. The office was full of vines growing all over the walls. Perry sat there, not quite sure what to say.

"Perry, you have been a good assistant all year and only recently your attitude has changed around me. I think I know why, but I want to hear your side of the story and clear up any bad leaves between us."

Perry stared around at the office of plants. "My uncle was a citizen of colony J and it still bothers me that you killed them. I want to work with you but my father says no. I'm so conflicted."

Dr. Fogg nodded his head. "You're right. I will not deny that you shouldn't be okay with what I have done. But you need to understand these things about me. I have a condition that makes it very hard for me to control myself around my plants. I love them like people, like my family and to see them hurt really triggers my anger. You can hate me all you want and you don't have to trust me. But I see a passion for plants in your eyes and your fleet admiral knows how much knowledge is in my head. You would benefit a lot from what I and no one else can teach you. Also in case you didn't know this position will be full time but not like what you have been doing the last few months. Some of it will be, but I might send you on errands and you will get to travel and pick up plants and seeds for me."

Perry sat there with his hand shaking. On one hand he wanted to work with plants, he wanted to know everything. But learning from a man who committed genocide and murder, Perry's stomach felt uneasy.

"Perry, I'm not going to force your hand. But you would be doing a great service. You have seen what I can do in six months with the resources I have. Imagine what we can do with if we have more. Perry I don't get to go out. I have a microchip in my ankle and if I go any further than the roof or that front door I get a horrible shock through my body and only approved people are allowed to visit me. I love my plants more than anything but my life is really lonely. These last few months have reminded me of what it is like to have human contact. When I saw you and your love for plants, I knew you were the one to ask. I can always find somebody else if you have too much of an issue. But you are one person I would trust with my plants."

Perry sat there quiet for a moment. "My dad is coming for a visit in a few days. Can the decision wait until I talk to him?"

"Your dad, you say? Well that will be interesting." Dr. Fogg smiled. "You take all the time you need."

Perry stood up. "James I don't want you to think I'm ungrateful or anything. This is an amazing opportunity it is just that it's a very hard decision for me to make."

"I'm sure in the end you will make the right choice." James stood up. "I have nothing but confidence in you." He walked over to Perry, placing his hand on his shoulder.

***

Perry's feelings of uneasiness didn't go away. He sat in the cafeteria picking at his butter chicken and pondering the moral decision he was about to make.

"Hey Perry, what are you doing in the cafeteria? Don't you eat lunch with the plants?" Skyler placed his tray down next to Perry's.

Perry let out a sigh. "I don't feel right going back there when I don't need to right now."

Skyler sat down. "Why not, you love plants. It's almost like you think they are real people or something?"

"Some are sentient, you know that right? There're even plant based life forms in the Forces. But that's not it. I do love plants, just..." Perry picked at his butter chicken. "It's just the offer to be James's assistant. I want to be, but I don't know if I can."

Skyler had a mouthful of seafood pasta, "Take the job. You get to play with plants for the rest of your life. What's the big deal?"

"It's until I graduate. Then I'm going to get a posting back to my colony. But this is the man who murdered my family. He is a monster. But he has a lot to offer."

"I'm pretty certain he's not going to murder you. What's the big deal? He is harmless now. Take his knowledge before it is wasted." Skyler said.

"He's a monster. This isn't an easy decision." Perry stared down at his food.

"With knowledge comes responsibility. He might be a monster, but you have morals and a heart. You know not to use your love of plants against people. So, learn what he has to offer and don't follow in his footsteps." Skyler dug at more of his food.

"Before I knew this I would have said yes. This is my dream job. I would love to live in a greenhouse." Perry began to sulk.

"Do it, then. You have a good career opportunity here, and you have a girlfriend. I think for the next 3 years this could be a good home for you. I'm hoping to stay here too, it's a lot better than Earth." Skyler replied. "Maybe with what you learned from James you can help undo his negative."

"My dad is coming tonight I'll talk to him. But you have helped me with your suggestions." Perry finished his food and got up.

***

Skyler was walking down the hall when he got a message on his communicator from Cane telling him to meet him in his office. He skipped class and went to the office. He knocked on the door. "Cane, you wanted to see me?"

Cane gestured for Skyler to sit down. He poured a drink then let out a deep sigh. "I got some bad news."

Skyler raised an eyebrow. "What do you mean, sir?"

"The charges against you are pretty serious especially with your past record on Squall and not being from this world. I tried to talk to Kreeve about it, he is willing to drop the charges but he wants something I can't just give him. We have to appear in court tomorrow. To discuss what they are going to do and when we meet again."

Skyler sighed. "I hate this guy and believe he deserves more of a beating than what I gave him. But what does he want? I mean if it will get him to drop the charges and prevent me having jail time, what does he want?"

Cane let out a deep sigh. "You're not going to like this. He wants me to let him keep his full pension and retire him without penalty."

Skyler stayed silent for a moment. "I love Kax and he did horrible things to her. How many others has he done things to? I think I am going to have to fight it."

"I thought you would say that. I have gotten you the best lawyer I can get for tomorrow but we know you're guilty so let's make sure we can get you a reduced sentence so that you are not in jail, maybe just community service. Also tomorrow I need you to be on your best behavior. No outbursts of any kind, understood?"

Skyler nodded his head. "Right, I can do that."

Chapter 25

Perry was making his way down to the loading dock when he saw Kax in the distance. He waved to her and called out, "Hey Kax!"

Kax stopped in her tracks and turned to face Perry. "Hey Perry, how are you doing? I thought you were working with plants?"

Perry scratched his head. "I was, but Dr. Fogg gave me a couple of days off to have time with my dad. I was heading to the loading dock to go and pick him up. What are you doing here?"

"I'm heading to class. I'm a pilot remember? The loading dock is near the flight hangar. I don't go through the main doors of the hangar because our section is at the back so we go through the back door." Kax sighed. "I know what I was doing was wrong but I enjoyed class then. I really wish they would change the instructor. Cane said I didn't have to go but I really enjoy flying and learning."

Perry raised an eyebrow, "Ya Skyler has court today because of it. He really cares about you."

Kax's eyes widened, "What? Court? Why is he in court? Because he beat Kreeve up? Why didn't he tell me?"

Perry shrugged. "He probably didn't want you to worry about him. It's just a small court date to decide if they're going forward or not."

"Have they left yet?" Kax asked in a panic.

Perry looked at his watch, "It's 6 a.m. I think there is time to still catch them."

Kax rushed down the hall. "Thank you Perry. I still have time."

Perry watched as Kax disappeared out of sight.

He sat on the bench near the loading dock waiting for the ship to arrive. He was early but it didn't bother him. His main concern was seeing his dad and deciding what to do. While he sat on the bench, he pulled out his pocket tablet and started to work out formulas for new plants. The time passed and before he knew it he heard a gruff cough come from in front of him.

Perry picked up his head and saw his dad standing in front of him. He moved his head side to side and noticed the platform was empty. "Where is everyone?"

His dad laughed. "The ship arrived and everyone has left. I have been standing in front of you this whole time. You were too focused on your work you didn't notice. Let me guess, more plant stuff?"

A look of guilt crossed over Perry's face. "I'm sorry, Dad. I didn't mean to. I got here early and decided to do some work. I think I have a way to grow grass in a desert without water. There is this type of grass seed from Milo 5 that feeds on the heat. It only requires moisture to germinate never again. But it needed to be adapted to Earth's oxygen…"

"That's great, son, but you know I have no interest in plants just tell me when your plants save the world." His dad held up his brown leather carrying bag. "Now if we're done with plants can we put my bags somewhere?"

Perry saved his work and put away his pocket tablet and led his dad down the hall.

Perry's father had blonde hair with streaks of white, dark brown eyes and pale complexion. Perry never looked much like his father. He took after his mother more. He walked with his dad to the visitor's quarters. They got to the front desk and signed in. Perry took the key and walked his father down the hall. The room was like a small apartment: there was a small kitchenette, a couch, a double bed, and a full bathroom.

"This place is nicer than the one on Earth. They have shared bathrooms down the halls for the guest." Perry's dad put his suitcase down on the bed. "How far is your room from here?"

Perry paused to think. "It's actually pretty far from here. But normally I'm not in there. I have been camping in the greenhouse most of the time. But James has given me a few days off."

His father raised an eyebrow as he unzipped his suitcase, "You have been staying in the same room as this doctor too? What is going on? How serious are you about this apprentice thing?"

"Assistant dad, I'll be his assistant. I have not been sharing a room I have a cot in one of the climate control rooms. But that's only for naps. With the sun schedule sometimes we only have time to nap a little before we got to go out again." Perry paused. "As for how serious I am, well, I can learn tons of skills from James that I can't learn from anyone else. Also I will have access to really rare plants. It's only for a few years then I will graduate and return home to the colon..."

"And commit genocide on all of us?" His father butted in.

Perry stood there mortified. "NO! I love the colony! I want to have a job where I can work and live there. I want to raise a family there. The colony is my home. But with these skills I'm learning maybe I can find a way to make the colonies self sufficient in case anything happens to Earth in the war. Dad I'm not Dr. Fogg. I want to help."

His dad sat on the bed and patted the bed next to him, "Come sit down next to me Perry."

Perry took a seat next to his father. He rubbed his hands around each other, nervous what his father might say.

"Son I love you and I think you're a very smart boy. I don't understand much about your plants but I know you want to learn," He put his hand on his son's shoulder and looked into his eyes. "I just worry you are very susceptible. You have already changed since you joined the Forces. You drink and have an alien girlfriend and get into bar fights. You're turning into someone I don't recognize and I worry you will change and this Dr. Fogg will corrupt you and turn you against what you love."

Perry shook his head, "Dad, that won't happen. Yes I have changed but it's called growing up, Dad. I'm on my own and I was only in one fight. I will not change my values. I know what is right and wrong. I don't support genocide and I want to use his knowledge to help people."

"Well I brought you the articles I have on Dr. Fogg. I kept them after your uncle died. It sickens me that man is still alive. Stay safe."

"Dad you know I will." Perry said with a soft smile.

His father rubbed his shoulder. "Are there any rules about you staying on the couch bed while I visit?"

Perry shook his head. "I don't think so I'll spend as much time as I can with you dad. I can't wait for you to meet Stellik and my friends. You will like them."

Chapter 26

Skyler sat in the courtroom. He was in his dress uniform. Next to him was Cane. He fidgeted sitting there. Cane had told him to be quiet while they waited for everyone to arrive. The Catillion prosecutors were right on time, and talked amongst themselves for several minutes.

Skyler looked around the small courtroom. *Hmm, Kreeve hasn't arrived yet? Isn't he supposed to be here too?*

It wasn't much longer before a man in a well fitted blue suit came rushing through the door. He came to the table where Skyler and Cane were sitting. He held out his hand, "Hello there! I'm Attorney Iolaus Stormwell. You, I guess, are Skyler Therris?"

Skyler shook the ash blonde attorney's hand. "Why, yes I am. You're human, what are you doing out here if you're a civilian lawyer?"

Iolaus laughed. "What can I say, I like cats. We can discuss more of this after court. Right now we need to discuss if we are wanting to go forward. Cane has filled me in on the situation."

Skyler nodded, "Okay sounds good to me. When is court starting?"

The lawyer looked at his watch, "Should have been just before I got here. I wonder why the others haven't arrived yet."

A moment later Kreeve and his lawyer walked in the doors. They sat at the table next to Skyler.

Skyler tried to avoid looking at Kreeve. The sight of him filled him with rage.

It wasn't long before court started. They all rose for the judge. The judge sat down and they all copied. The judge flipped through the papers in front of him. "Today we are here to discuss the assault charges on Skyler Therris. How do you plead?"

Iolaus stood up and straightened his suit he was about to speak when the other guy's attorney stood up and said. "I'm sorry your honor, but my client has just informed me that he will not be testifying against Mr. Therris."

All the eyes were on Kreeve and his attorney. The prosecutors were muttering to themselves fretfully.

"Is that so?" said the judge. "Your client was very badly beaten and he now wants to drop everything?"

The attorney looked at Kreeve and received a nod. "Yes, that is correct, your honor."

The judge looked to the Catillion prosecutors. "Does this affect the case you are prepared to bring?"

The prosecutors conferred for a moment, and one of them turned to the judge.

"If Mr. Kreeve will not testify," he said, "we will not be proceeding with the charge."

"Well then, in that case, no further need to be here. The charge is dismissed and I will issue an order to that effect." The judge banged his gavel.

They all stood up. Skyler turned to Cane, "What was that about?"

Cane looked over Skyler's shoulder, "I have no idea but something's going on with him."

Iolaus finished packing up his things, "Well, I'd call that a success. My afternoon's free now. Want to go catch some drinks and celebrate? First round's on me as soon as I get your bill done up."

Skyler paused, *I already have the day off school. Drinks would be great...but what made him change his mind?* Skyler looked at Cane. "I'm down for drinks."

Cane checked his watch. "Well, we did end earlier than expected; I guess a round or two will be fine."

Iolaus made a fist and cheered. "All right, then. Let's get going."

***

Skyler got back to the academy. He had more than a few drinks and stumbled to his room. When he got to the door he saw Kax waiting outside. He stopped. "Kax, why are you sitting outside the room?"

When she saw Skyler she jumped up and gave him a hug. Her face was covered in tears, "Oh Skyler, there you are. I was so worried." She hugged him tighter.

Skyler patted her back. "What's wrong Kax? You know I will always be fine."

She buried her face into him. "No, not this time. Things were going to go really south and I had to do it. I had to save you. I tried calling you but you didn't answer your phone."

Skyler pulled his communicator out of his pocket and saw several missed calls. He lightly pushed Kax off him. "What did you do? Let's go to my room and talk about it." With Kax out of his arms he unlocked the door and headed in. He went over to the mini fridge on Perry's side of the room and grabbed out a self-labeled bottle of 'vitamin water' and took a sip before putting it back in.

Kax sat on his bed, "What did you just do?"

Skyler smiled. "I discovered a few weeks ago this vitamin water Perry has for the plants is great for sobering up. He doesn't know I drink it, I thought it was vodka one night and, well, this is now our little secret."

"I would tell Perry what you have been drinking," Kax said. "It might not be safe."

Skyler scoffed and went and sat next to Kax on the bed. "So what has got you so upset? What did you do?" He put his arm around her to comfort her.

Kax put her hands in her face. "I got your charges dropped. He did drop the charges, right?"

Skyler's eyes widened and his tone became serious. "What did you do, Kax?"

She looked right into Skyler's eyes. "This morning I heard you were going to court and I knew that Kreeve was going to stop at nothing to ruin you. I know you had been trying with Cane but nothing was working. So before court this morning I went to see Kreeve and talked to him."

Skyler moved back. "Kax, you didn't."

"I was going to do whatever it took to get those charges dropped." She paused. "I went to his room and asked him nicely to drop the charges and he said no. He was about to leave and out of nowhere I blurted out I was pregnant."

Skyler's hands shook and his heart stopped. "You can't be, please tell me you're lying!" His heart was starting to race and he could feel the beads of sweat on his forehead.

"Of course not, Skyler. I'm definitely not!" She snapped back. "But I told him that because I knew he wouldn't want to draw more attention to this and definitely wouldn't want the bastard of one of his students running around."

Skyler took a deep breath and calmed down. "So what, now he thinks you're pregnant?"

"Well, sort of. I told him that if he dropped the charges I would abort the baby."

A disgusted look crossed Skyler's face. "Why would you do that! That's a horrible thing to do, bargain a baby's life."

A tear came to Kax's eye. "There is no child so I was just bluffing. You were willing to give your life up for mine."

Skyler sighed, "Ya I know I was. Thank you for getting the charges dropped. It really does mean a lot to me. Just as an unwanted child, I don't like hearing about getting rid of children."

"I get it, Skyler, and you must know if there was a child, I wouldn't have said these things. I'm sorry to upset you." Kax put her hand on Skyler's shoulder.

He leaned over and gave her a hug. They held each other in their arms for a moment. Skyler broke the hug, "Wait how are you going to prove this to him? He just took your word for it?"

Kax shook her head, "I borrowed the ultrasound photos from a classmate. There is another girl who is pregnant in my program."

Skyler was shaking a bit. "And how are you going to prove you ended it?"

"Make a fake doctor's note, as long as there is no baby I don't think he will care." Kax sighed, "Skyler, I know it wasn't right what I did but I didn't see a choice. I had to help you."

Skyler closed his eyes and held her tight. "It's fine. Let's just move past it and agree not to be so reckless again, okay?"

Kax nodded her head, "Okay, I can agree to that."

***

Skyler banged on the door with a bottle in his hand. "Perry, you better be in there!"

An older blonde haired man answered the door. "Who do you think you are, making such racket?"

Skyler smelled of alcohol and stretched his neck to look over the man's shoulder. "Is Perry in there?"

Perry was sitting on the bed looking at the news articles. "Dad, it's okay, that's just Skyler."

Perry's father stepped aside and let the drunk Skyler in.

Skyler waltzed over to the bed and flopped down with a wine bottle in his hand. "Perry stop worrying about books. Let's go out and celebrate my freedom!"

Perry moved the articles aside and narrowed his eyes at Skyler. "You're already drunk. Why do we need to do more celebrating? You know my Dad is here."

Skyler looked at Perry with sad eyes, "He can come too if he wants."

Perry sighed and turned his focus to his dad. "Dad, I won't be out all night. I think Skyler needs me."

His father groaned, "Fine, but be safe. I'm locking the door at one so you better be back before then."

Perry helped Skyler off the bed and dragged him out of the room. "What is going on, Skyler? You knew my Dad was here. I haven't seen him in two years. Why are you ruining my time with him?"

Skyler slid down onto the floor. "Sorry I keep screwing up no matter where I go and I should be celebrating the charges were dropped but my reckless attitude is just getting people in more trouble." He took a sip of wine.

Perry took the bottle away from Skyler and sat down next to him in the hallway. "What happened?"

Skyler placed his head between his knees, "Kax faked a pregnancy so that Kreeve would drop the charges. I'm such an idiot I shouldn't have gotten involved. I let my emotions get the better of me."

Perry placed his hand on Skyler's shoulder. "After what he did to Kax he deserved what you did to him. You just picked the wrong place to do it."

"I know he got what he deserved but what's upsetting me is I did more damage because of my reckless attitude." He began to cry, "I just wanted to protect Kax. I never wanted her to get hurt. I love her."

Perry patted Skyler on the back. "I have never been in love but I have seen it and I know you care about Kax and she knows that. I think the reason she lied to Kreeve was because on some level she cares about you too. What if it didn't work? What if he did worse to her? She was willing to take that risk to save you just as you were willing to risk everything for her."

"I guess it all did work out in the end. Just got to take it as a reason to think twice."

Perry stood up and held out his hand to help Skyler up. "You could always be a little bit more mature. I think you need to sleep. Go to your room and get a good night's sleep."

Skyler dusted himself off. "I guess you're right, you're always right Perry, you're so smart, you are always there for me when I need you." Skyler leaned in and kissed Perry on the lips.

Perry's eyes widened and pushed Skyler back. "Skyler I think you need to go back to your room now and get some sleep."

Skyler brushed the hair behind Perry's ear back. "I'll see you tomorrow."

Perry waved goodbye to Skyler, as he watched Skyler walk away he took a sip of the wine he had in his hand and went back into the room to finish the night with his father.

Chapter 27

Skyler awoke in the morning with an aching head. There was a knock on the door. Skyler grabbed his head and let out a screech. "Stop knocking my head hurts!" The knocking continued.

Skyler got out of bed and opened the door. Michael was standing on the other side. "What are you doing here?"

"You are late. Dr. Fogg is looking for you. We need the extra hand with the plants." Michael stared at Skyler.

Skyler rubbed his head. "Sorry I had court yesterday and I went drinking and well I didn't stop. It wasn't a good day."

Michael stepped into the room. "Did everything go okay? Are you really at risk of losing your career?"

Skyler grabbed his clothes off the floor. "No, the charges were dropped. Just some other stressful things happened is all. What do we need to do today with the plants? I thought we were waiting for the next growth cycle."

Michael shook his head, "That one is already done. We have a few going at the same time, so come on, get your pants on and let's get going. Take a hangover pill."

Skyler sat up in his bed and rubbed his head. "Sometimes I want to suffer with the hangover. It helps distract me from my emotional pain."

Michael clapped his hands. "Stop stalling. You know how Dr. Fogg is."

Skyler got out of bed and began to get dressed. "You're worse than my mother."

Michael picked up Skyler's cadet jacket off the floor and threw it at him. "You know that is not true."

Once Skyler finished getting dressed the two men rushed to the greenhouse. Dr. Fogg was waiting for them by the newly full grown plants. "Skyler, you're late." He picked up a dish of berries. "I assume you have another hangover. Please take one of these berries. They will help."

Skyler narrowed his eyes towards Fogg, "No thank you and I won't be late again."

Dr. Fogg put the bowl of berries down. "You're smarter than you look. You weren't that late so no harm was done. You don't have to eat one. If you actually caused damage, well, that's a different story." He continued to stroll over and grab one of the pots. "Come on boys, grab a plant and let's get working."

Skyler and Michael both grabbed a plant. Skyler whispered to Michael, "Are those berries what I think they are?"

Michael carried his plant, "I think it is a good warning, proving James has not changed. Never touch those berries."

Skyler peered over his shoulder at the round dish of berries gaining an uneasy feeling from its sight.

***

It was night once again and Skyler was covered in dirt and was heading back to the dorms for a shower when Kax passed by in the hall. Skyler waved to Kax. "Hey, coming back from having a shower? I was just about to have one."

Kax was holding her purple towel in her arms. "Yeah, I just finished. Long day at the lab?"

Skyler rubbed his forehead unintentionally, smearing the mud on his forehead. "Ya, especially after yesterday. I want to apologize about yesterday I was drunk and it was really emotional. I shouldn't have kissed you after what happened."

Kax's eyebrow raised and her ears twitched, "You didn't kiss me. We hugged but that was it. We agreed to give each other space. You left and I didn't see you until now."

Skyler tilted his head, "I remember vividly making out with someone. Who else did I talk to?" He brushed his hair back.

Kax shrugged. "I don't know, but I would check your messages. Perry has invited us all out tonight to meet his dad."

Skyler's eyes widened, his memories returned. "I got to go. I'll see you tonight." Before Kax could reply Skyler ran down the halls to the guest wing. Skyler knocked on Perry's dad's door. Perry answered the door this time.

"Skyler, you're covered in dirt what's going on?" Perry asked.

Skyler panting, tried to catch his breath. "Perry, what happened last night? I thought I went drinking and made out with Kax. Then I talked to her but she said no. What happened when I saw you?"

Perry shrugged, "You got the events backwards. You made out with me. You were really drunk, but it is understandable no big deal."

Skyler raised an eyebrow, "What do you mean it's understandable? Perry I'm sorry."

"No need to apologize, you were drunk and upset. It is not the first time." Perry brushed off the apology.

Skyler was taken aback by Perry's comment. "What! What do you mean? I have kissed you before?"

Perry rolled his eyes, "You really forget every time? I'm not sure how to take that. But yes, a handful of times you have gotten seriously drunk and kissed me. I thought you were bi all this time. Remember that threesome we were in? You kissed me there and got a little too close to me."

Skyler brushed his hair back and rubbed his forehead, unsure how to respond. "Do I really get that drunk? I mean you are cute, it's just I'm shocked that I get that drunk."

Perry put his hand on Skyler's shoulder, "Drinking a lot is an understatement. There have been times I have been worried about your life like when this school year started. Are you bisexual? I know you have kissed me, but I have never seen you with a guy unless something is going on between you and Michael?"

Skyler sat down on the concrete floor rubbing his head. "Nothing is going on with me and Michael. But as far as being bisexual, I don't know. I have never been that fond of guys but in high school I was in a triad with my friend Paul and our girlfriend, Xandria. Me and Paul did a couple of things together but we split because Xandria and Paul got married and I joined the academy. But when it comes to my experience with men, I don't have much. Women catch my attention more. That's why I never considered myself to like men. Perry, I'm sorry if I have made you feel uncomfortable."

Perry sat down next to Skyler on the floor. "It doesn't bother me, I'm open minded, willing to try new things. If it did I would have told you the first time. Since I met you three years ago you have introduced me to a lot of new things. Life on the colonies is all monogamous and lifelong mates. Not that we are forced to conform, just our populations are low and there are only so many families. Me and my high school girlfriend have grown so far apart I'm hoping to bring someone back with me when I graduate."

Skyler sat there thinking about his life and times he had encountered situations with men and what his sexuality really was. *Is it just I get disoriented or do I really find men attractive? Never really thought about it. Perry is cute.* "Perry, let me know if this is crossing a line but to test a theory could I kiss you?"

Perry laughed. "Dude, it doesn't bother me at all. I will gladly help you figure out your sexuality."

Skyler leaned over and kissed Perry on the lips. He kissed him passionately and for a moment their lips locked.

When they separated Perry looked at Skyler, "so how was it having a sober male kiss?"

"It was just like any other kiss. And you are a good kisser." Skyler kissed Perry again. This time pushing him onto the floor and feeling his body up.

Perry pushed him off. "Stop. We're in the hallway, you need a shower and-"

"I get it, Perry, we will continue this conversation later." Skyler got up and dusted himself off.

"See you tonight for dinner. My dad is looking forward to meeting my friends." Perry picked himself off the floor and dusted himself off. "See you soon."

Skyler waved goodbye and headed down the hall. He went down the halls of the buildings making his way back to his room. *Could I really be interested in men? It's not something I really thought about. I am attracted to Perry, he is cute. Maybe I should give Paul a call and talk about these new feelings, he'll know what to say. It's been a while since we talked.*

***

Perry was ready to go. He was running a comb through his hair one more time before it was time to go out for dinner. There was a knock on the door. Perry went over and Kax was standing there in a pair of black slim pants and hot pink t-shirt. "Hey Perry, I'm here!" She said.

Perry stepped outside of the room into the hall. "Hey Kax, it is great to see you. Can we talk for a moment?"

Kax shrugged and cheerfully replied. "Sure, what is going on, Perry?"

Perry rubbed the back of his neck. "I don't know if I should be telling you this but Skyler and I made out."

Kax's eyes popped. "Our friend Skyler? The one who is always hitting on me? I don't understand?"

"I know and Skyler would probably want to tell you on his own time when he figures everything out. But I need to figure things out." Perry sighed. "I need to talk to someone about me figuring things out. Damn, why is everything falling on me? I don't have time to figure out people's sexuality while dealing with my future career."

Kax gave Perry a hug. "Do you like Skyler?"

Perry held her close. "I don't know, I don't think so, not in the way he likes me. I barely know when I like a girl. Like really like a girl." He broke the hug. "I worry because I think he liked it more than me and I said I would help him and I don't know what to do. I have-"

Kax put her finger in front of his mouth. "Shh, you don't need to sleep with Skyler. If this is bothering you this much you clearly don't share the same feelings. If he bugs you about it, tell him. It's easy saying no to Skyler."

Perry laughed, "You do have a lot of experience doing that. Thank you for this. I just have had a lot to process."

Michael and Skyler soon came from down the hall. They waved to Perry, "Hey buddy we're here. Ready to go?" Skyler said.

Perry waved back to them, "Great I will get my dad and we can get going."

"Where are we going to eat?" Michael asked.

"Just the base's restaurant, we will be walking there. So don't worry about your diet Michael." Perry opened the door to the room, "Hey dad we're all here, ready to go?"

Perry's father came to the door with a portfolio in his hand, "I'm ready to go. I'm looking forward to meeting your friends properly." He shot a glare at Skyler.

"Well if we are all ready, let's get going." Perry said, keeping a cheery smile.

They made their way to the base's restaurant. Perry had reservations and were guided to a booth in the back. On one side Skyler and Kax sat next to each other and Michael sat next to Perry and his father on the other side.

The waitress came by with the menus and some water. Perry pointed to his dad. "So everyone this is my dad, Richard. As you know he is visiting from colony H."

His dad waved to everyone.

Perry pointed to his friends one by one. "That's Kax, Skyler and Michael. Kax is a pilot, Michael is the engineer who I have been working with. And Skyler, well, he is the command cadet and my roommate."

A little while later the waitress came and took their orders. They enjoyed their food and during the meal Skyler blurted out, "hey Richard, what is in the folder you brought?"

"Interesting you should ask," Richard said. He placed the folder on the table between the food and opened it up. "It is the info Perry asked for about James Fogg."

Skyler raised a brow.

Perry choked on his water. "Dad, you brought that here? You already showed me some pages on him. Why did you bring it to my friends?"

"Because you have told me that Skyler and Michael have been working for this monster. They should all know what he has done." Richard said.

"Dad, this is a public place!" Perry whispered loudly.

Michael took the papers and looked them over. "Perry it will be fine. These are all from newspapers. This info is public, and there are not many people this far back in the restaurant."

Perry took a bite of his food, disgruntled.

"What do the articles say, Michael?" Skyler asked.

Michael read over a few more papers. "James really has issues. The genocide is only part of the story. When they took him into custody he attacked the cops for what it says here, 'they touched my plants.' I know that he has threatened to hurt us if we hurt them and warned you but this was not like a punch, this was stabbing."

Kax grabbed one of the articles, "This is his mental health analysis. He failed in every part. But according to this doctor's notes it is always related to plants. When they tested him when he had a plant in his hands he was fine. I think this guy is dangerous."

Skyler finished the sip of his beer. "But that's the thing, Cane looked over these things and he made sure that he is on strict watch and is always with plants so he has been neutralized."

"You can never neutralize a monster like that." Richard said.

Kax took a piece of paper, "Was the genocide successful?"

Richard put his head down, "Yes it was. Well, with one of the colonies, but he didn't get to the others. This man is not well."

Perry took a deep breath and put down his fork. "Dad, I have the opportunity to learn about plants from one of the most brilliant minds or I could hope to learn close to what he knows from books. I'm confused by what you're trying to do, Dad. I know the risks and how I see it working with a mentally unstable guy is safer than some of the postings I could get. At least I knows what plants are poisonous. Are you telling me what to do or going to let me make my own decision?"

The whole table stopped and looked towards Richard. Richard paused. "I might be your father but you are an adult. I would love to tell you no and bring you back home, but I understand you're an adult. I just want to provide you with the info before you side with this man."

All eyes were on Perry. Perry took a sip of his water, "I will get back to you. I need to think but until then I would prefer to not talk about him for the rest of the trip."

They all handed the papers back to Richard and they were placed back into the folder. The table remained silent.

Skyler put his fork down, "Hey Perry, where is your girlfriend? Why isn't she at this dinner?"

Richard turned his glance at Perry, "This girl Kax isn't your girlfriend?"

Kax stared at Perry and he rubbed his neck, "She has to work late tonight and we're going to have dinner with her tomorrow. Kax is just a friend, not even the same race as Stellik."

"I'm sorry, most aliens do look the same to me. I know aliens are different than humans but the colony is a human colony. The aliens are all the ones who have moved in and work on the colony or have stopovers." Perry's father said.

Perry covered his face. "Dad, you can't say things like that. Ugh."

Michael cut in. "Sir in all due respect I have met many people who are ignorant of other life forms in my life, but while I have you here I feel it is an obligation to enlighten you." He pushed his hair back to reveal his unpointed ears. "Notice my ears, oval eyes, flat bridged nose and I am not sure if you paid attention to my height when we came in but I am taller than most humans. I am what is called a Squallite. I am the race you probably commonly see working on the colony. Now Kax next to me is a Catillion, you see her ears have fur and are on top of her head and she has gold eyes with diamond pupils. I hope you can see the difference. I understand you may not have seen her race often outside of the planet but mine I'm sure you have. I hope you have learnt from this experience."

The table went quiet. All eyes were on Perry's father. He took a sip of his drink then replied, "Thank you for your information. I will keep that in mind for the future." He shifted in his seat towards Perry, "So your girlfriend is a Squallite?"

Perry nodded his head, "Yes father, she is, and an officer and older than me. She is becoming someone special to me."

"I knew the day you left the colonies you would come home with an alien girlfriend. Your sister is dating a green skinned named Grik or something? She only told me about him. I didn't get to meet him."

"I have seen him on the holo phone a few times, he is nice but I don't think the two of them are that serious." Perry commented.

"Good, because she has lots of men interested in her back home."

Perry saw his beer was dry, reached over and took a sip of Skyler's beer. "Dad, are we really going to talk about this now? The colony was considered a success and the new generation can marry outside and bring new people in or leave. Also Dad, sis just joined the Forces. She's got a few years before she decides where she is going. Can we just enjoy dinner tonight?"

Richard picked up his fork, "As you wish."

Skyler waved to the waitress and ordered another round of beers for the table.

Chapter 28

Perry walked down the hall and with a heavy heart and pounding head from the hangover from the night before. He hesitated as he was about to knock on the door. *What am I doing? I should just let it be and not say anything. No, no it is not fair. I haven't seen her, and she needs to know what is going on and decide for herself if she wants to continue things with me.* He knocked on the door.

Stellik answered the door. "Perry, what are you doing here? I thought we were meeting tonight for dinner."

Perry sighed, "We were, but I need to talk to you before dinner, if that is okay?"

She stepped aside from the door and let Perry in. "Come in sit down and we will have some orange tea."

Perry took a seat at the table and sat there quietly until the tea was ready.

"Perry, I know you have a hangover. I can see it in your eyes but why are you so quiet?" She came over with two mugs of tea. "What is going on with you?"

Perry took a sip of his tea. "Where do you see our relationship going?"

"Wherever you want it to go. I care about you, but I understand I'm a Squallite, you're human, and the age gap is quite big for you humans." She took the seat across from Perry.

"It has nothing to do with you. It's all me. And if you wish to continue things with me after I tell you everything then I would be happy if you still wanted me, but I'll understand if not." He took a sip of his tea. "I know we met in the oddest of circumstances but I have grown to like you and enjoy you in the past few months but lots has changed. My buddy Skyler has recently discovered he is bisexual and has a crush on me. We made out yesterday. He was more into than I was. And I love my dad and he taught me to love the colony and my home but he is a little too much of an alien racist. There aren't many aliens on the colony and I have only been newly exposed with them in the past couple of years. I have no issue but I didn't realize how much of an issue he has. He isn't violent or telling me to break up with you but he would prefer me and my sister to date humans."

She held Perry's hand. "I'm a Squallite in the United Galactic Forces. I know what racism is and I have grown to accept people are going to think what they want to about me. I like you a lot, Perry. I think you're sweet and this age gap doesn't bother me because Squallites live to be 200. Now the only thing that gets me is you and Skyler. I mean, are you looking to pursue anything with him?"

Perry rubbed his head. "I like the guy, as a friend. We have been in threesomes together and shared a bed and I mean it isn't far off. But I think going any further is too far for me. I like him but he is a friend. I'll help him find someone but it's not me. And now just so you know I didn't try to make out with him. He had been drunk the night before and made out with me and when he was sober he realized who he made out with and apologized. I told him it was okay and then he asked if he could kiss me again to see if he liked it when sober and I agreed. I didn't intend to cheat on you, if that's how you want to see it. I mean are we together? We have seen each other a few times over the past few months and you are steady in my life. I like you a lot and I want you to meet my friends and family." Perry buried his face in his hands.

She leaned over and rubbed Perry's shoulder. "I like you too and I think we have a good thing. You didn't do anything wrong with Skyler, I understand. If your dad is such a racist as you say then he doesn't bother me. I know you aren't and that's all that matters to me, okay cutie? I'm used to human racism."

Perry raised his head and smiled at her. "Thank you for understanding. You mean a lot to me. This isn't where I thought I would be 5 years ago but I feel that since joining UGF my life has grown more colorful and I love it. I want this."

"Then I want you."

Chapter 29

"Perry, it's good to see you again, glad to have you back." Dr. Fogg lifted his head up from the plant he was grooming.

Perry walked further into the greenhouse and picked up a set of clippers off the workstation desk and headed towards Dr. Fogg. "Yeah I'm back, and I'm going to be staying until I graduate."

Dr. Fogg raised an eyebrow, "Oh, you have plans for after you graduate?"

Perry clipped a dead leaf off a plant. "I'm going back home to the colony. I have talked to Cane about this plan and he is going to see what he can do for me." He concentrated on the plants, not looking at Fogg.

Fogg walked up behind Perry and peered over his shoulder. "Be careful with the plants."

Perry tensed and jumped, dropping the clippers. He turned and stared at Dr. Fogg. "What are you doing?"

Dr. Fogg stared at him, "What's with the attitude? You returned to me but you're not comfortable being here?"

Perry walked over to the end of the row of plants and sat down in the folding chair. He put his head in his hands. "James, I want to work and learn about plants and you're the best person to do so with, but I have just learnt so much about you."

"If you still have this issue with me, why did you agree to come back? The facts in those articles are true but you know me personally. You know I will not hurt you. If you hurt my plants without a good scientific reason, yes I will hurt you, but otherwise you know you are safe." Fogg said standing from a distance.

Perry let out a deep sigh, "I know, and you know I would never hurt a plant. It's just with the new knowledge it is hard to go back to what we had. But I want to try."

Dr. Fogg looked at the clock on the wall. "Michael will be here soon. As a sign of good faith I will give you some space. I think in time things will get better."

Perry whispered under his breath, "I hope I made the right choice."

Michael and Skyler both arrived not long after. Skyler went over to Perry. He smiled and stood close to him. "I have been thinking about you."

Perry put his set of clippers down. "Skyler, we need to talk."

Skyler got that look in his eyes, "About what? Can I kiss you?"

Perry put his hand up. "No Skyler, stay back. I like you but we can't be anything more than just close friends. I'm not attracted to men and I don't think that's going to change. When we kissed, you felt something, I didn't. I'm willing to help you but nothing is happening between us. Also me and Stellik have become an official thing. She is my girlfriend now."

Skyler stopped and took a deep breath, "I see, well, that's disappointing. I mean she seems nice, just…I had an interest, that's what has made me disappointed."

Perry was unsure how to respond, "Um, I'm sorry. I will help you find someone if you want."

Skyler rubbed his neck, "I will see. I'm still figuring all of this out. I mean, I like you, but I was also hoping for someone who was a friend in case I'm not, how do we put this, ready to do it."

Perry placed his hand on Skyler's shoulder. "Skyler you helped me come out of my shell when we first met. I will help you and I will not let anything bad happen to you okay?"

Skyler smiled, "Thanks, buddy."

Dr. Fogg came over between the two. "Get back to clipping dead leaves this is the last harvest and these plants need to be perfect."

"This is the end already? I thought there were a few more tests?" Skyler asked.

"The last tests worked out well and we just had to grow a batch and it's ready to go. A demonstration will be held at the end of today." He turned his focus to Perry, "this is also where the fleet admiral will make the final decision on allowing you to be my assistant." Perry and Dr. Fogg stared at each other for a moment.

Skyler broke the tension between the two by saying, "So what is going to become of these plants if we complete these tests and they are approved?"

Dr. Fogg grinned at Skyler, "Simple, once they are all finally approved the fleet admirals will order more and then start training people on how to use them and their proper care. These will become as common as a gun on ships if all goes according to plan."

Perry's hand clenched with uneasiness thinking of all the things he had learnt about Fogg in the past few weeks. He wasn't sure if he should trust him with noxious gas plants. "How will these be stored on the ship? What if one of them falls over? Did we think of a way to protect the crew from an accidental leak?"

Skyler put his hand on Perry's shoulder to help him calm down. "Perry these things have already been thought of by the higher ups. The plants will be put in protective cases on the ships and these bean pods have to be crushed pretty hard to open. Safety precautions are already being put in place."

Perry took a deep breath. "Yeah I remember now, just so much has been going on I forgot about the meeting when we talked about the safety."

Skyler rubbed Perry's shoulder, "It's okay, buddy, you have been under a lot of stress. Come on, let's get these plants ready."

Perry and Skyler continued clipping and trimming the plants for hours, making sure they looked 100% perfect for when Cane arrived.

Just as they were finishing up, Fleet Admiral Cane, Admiral Ciccone and the Catillion Minister of Defence arrived. Perry, Skyler and Michael stood back while Dr. Fogg greeted the officials. "Welcome, it's so nice to have visitors."

"Shut up Fogg, the United Galactic forces is taking a big risk in trusting you. Cadets Zyrix and Jones is who we want to hear from." Said Admiral Ciccone. "Could you two please tell me and demonstrate to me how these plants work?"

Michael strode out of the simulator with a handful of gas masks. "The simulator is all set up and ready to go, when your ready admirals please put on these gas masks and follow me."

***

That night Perry and his friends went out partying to celebrate the success of the plants and Perry's new job as Dr. Fogg's assistant. While they were out Perry's father Richard made his way to the greenhouse. Richard knocked on the door. The door opened but there was no one standing on the other side. Richard walked in. "James Fogg, I'm here to talk to you. Come out and show your face, you coward!" The lights turned on and from the back of the greenhouse Dr. Fogg appeared.

"Richard Zyrix, we finally meet, you're here late. You do know I'm not supposed to have visitors right?" Dr. Fogg said.

"I think in this case, there will be an exception because you are training my son." Richard stepped towards Dr. Fogg.

"Right, you mean Perry." Dr. Fogg sat down on a folding chair. "What would you like to know?"

"I cannot control what my son does now that he is an adult, but I want you to know if you hurt him or corrupt him, I will come after you!" Richard stepped closer.

James raised his hand. "Do not come any closer, Mr. Zyrix. I know you are angry at me and I have taken the precaution of sitting near these lovely plants. They are quite protective of me and if you come any closer they will attack you."

"You never change. You are still the killer you were back then. You better not train my son to be anything like you!"

"I won't train your son to be anything. You are right, I haven't changed. That's why they keep me locked away on high doses of medication. But what keeps me alive is the knowledge in my mind. It might be rotten, but it is still a garden full of budding knowledge." Fogg took a deep breath. "If it puts your mind at ease, Perry is a good boy. I see nothing rotten in him. He will only gain knowledge from me. I do not teach how to kill. Any more concerns?"

Richard made a fist in frustration, "You took my brother away from me years ago and you took his family. I lend you Perry for these couple of years but you must promise to return him to me unharmed."

Dr. Fogg nodded his head. "I will return Perry in the condition he was given to me."

Chapter 30

Skyler heard a knock at his door and got up to answer it. "Hey Kandy, I'm so glad you came."

"Oh I'll be coming a lot tonight." Kandice said as she entered his room in a tan trench coat. She waited for Skyler to close the door before she opened her coat to reveal a sexy black negligee. "I was surprised you called me."

Skyler had a big smile on his face. "You look gorgeous but I didn't call you for this. You know we don't do that anymore."

She raised an eyebrow and sat down on the bed crossing her legs. "Then what is going on?"

Skyler took a deep breath, "I like guys."

She burst out laughing. "Skyler, we've had lots of sex. I know you like women."

"I mean…" he let out a big sigh, "I like women, but I have been dealing with my sexuality for a little while and I have quite recently come to the conclusion that there is no denying I also like guys."

"I can't say I'm surprised, but if you don't mind me asking, how did you not know this sooner?" Kandice asked.

Skyler sat down on Perry's bed, "My sex life is all touch and go. When I was younger it was the girls who approached me. It was easy to get chicks, I never really paid attention but I seem to form better bonds with guys. We grow closer and then I met Perry. There is something about him, he's adorable and charming and the one I would love to take the next step with him. Well I like him how I like girls. Kandy, I didn't have a father to teach me about women or men. Everything I know I have learnt from others. I have been going with the flow and repeating it, not stopping to think."

"What did he say about this?" Kandy asked, "also what does this mean about you and my sister?"

"We made out, but he isn't interested. I still like Kax a lot but I might have to accept something between us might not happen for a long time. I called you here because I needed someone to help me talk and work things out." Skyler rubbed his legs.

"Okay I get it, well for one thing, there is nothing wrong with you and not figuring it out sooner is okay. I mean I was the one who picked you up. I'm just as guilty for confusing you. But have there been other guys before, or are these feelings completely new?" Kandice asked.

Skyler shrugged, "I mean I guess there have. I have never slept with any but I have been comfortable around them when I'm intimate."

"Okay that's fine. So what do you want me to do about it? Why did you invite me over?" Kandice asked.

"I know Perry said he would help me out but I don't want to make him more uncomfortable. I also know you know how to find and pick up men. Maybe you could help me figure this out in a safe way."

She laughed. "You're cute and I think I know a couple of guys. I would be glad to help you out with this. Is that all? You want to do something? I'm half naked and sitting in front of you?"

Skyler laughed, "Kandy as much as that's tempting I couldn't. I still love Kax and it would just hurt her unless are you trying to use one of your tickets?"

She got off the bed, "I get it and it's fine. I don't want to use one of my tickets up right now, I might save it for a threesome with you and some guy but just random sex? Naw, there are plenty of men on base I could find tonight. Are Perry and Michael still single?"

Skyler stood up and headed to the door. "Perry has made it official with his girlfriend and Michael as always is asexual, so no chance hooking up with them."

She shrugged and made her way to the door, "That's fine there're other options."

Chapter 31

Skyler dialed an Earth phone number on the holo-phone. The operator kicked in, "It seems you are trying to reach a person on Earth in another galaxy. Extended long distance charades will apply. Press 1 to accept." Skyler pressed the button. The phone began to ring when a black haired man with glasses answered the call.

"Skyler, is that you?" said the man.

"It's great to see you again, Paul. It has been a long time." Skyler smiled.

"It's been like 4-5 years now? You should see little Logan, he is growing up so fast. I would show you but Xandria is out with the kids."

"Kids? You had another one? You and Xandria are still together?" Skyler asked.

Paul nodded, "Oh ya, our marriage is as strong and we have two Logan and Billy with a third on the way. Where are you now? you should come and visit and see the kids. Me and Xandria would love to see you again."

Skyler sighed, "I'm on Catillion for the next while. I don't know when I will be back. Especially with this war."

"Amazing, you really are going places in the Forces, aren't you? We moved north out of the city and out to Thunder Bay, it was more affordable and closer to Xandria's family. So there isn't much of the war up here. It might be far away form Rochester, but it's a lot safer."

"I'm really glad to hear that. I can't say I wasn't worried even if I haven't been in touch." Skyler put his head down.

"Skyler, I get it. Your path was going a different way than us and you weren't ready to be a father. So what is eating you? What made you call after all this time? I love hearing from you, but when you don't call for 4 years, I got to ask."

"You're right to ask. Paul, I called because I'm realizing some new things about myself and I wanted to know if you noticed anything because we used to be very close." Skyler paused, "I'm bisexual."

"It took you this long to figure it out?" Paul laughed. "Naw, I'm teasing. I know you didn't have it easy. But I always hoped you were, I was waiting for you to make a move."

"Ya, looking back at my teen years, I don't know how I didn't see it before. I wasn't good at picking people up when I was a teen they usually came to me." Skyler laughed.

"Skyler I don't know what to say to you besides…you be you. Follow your heart and I'm glad things are coming more clear to you. If you're ever in town me and Xandria would love to see you again and you can always join us like old times in high school." Paul winked.

"I will keep that in mind, there are some days I miss those days. You and Xandria made that time of my life bearable." Skyler smiled at Paul.

Just then Michael and Perry burst through the doors. "Skyler, where do you keep the good stuff? We have something to celebrate!" Perry said, rummaging though the desk.

Skyler turned in his chair, "First box under my bed. There is a bottle of Scotch, what's going on?"

"The plants were approved. We're geniuses! Our plants will be the new weapons on the ships. We did it!" Michael said with glee.

"That is amazing! Just one moment." Skyler turned back in his chair to Paul, "Paul I'm so sorry but I have got to go. I would love to talk to you again."

Paul smiled, "You guys have fun, I will tell Xandria you called. I hope to hear from you again."

Skyler waved goodbye and turned off the holo-phone.

Perry found the bottle, grabbed a couple of cleaned beakers from his side of the room and poured some Scotch into them and passed them around. "To plants and teamwork." They all took a beaker and toasted.

"Now we got the toast over, want to head to the bar? Let's not let this party end!" Perry cheered.

"Sounds great. I will call Kax and tell her to meet us there." Skyler pulled out his communicator.

Perry sealed the bottle and walked towards the door, "Tonight is going to be legendary!"

***

Skyler didn't stay out as late as the others. He kept checking his phone, there was no reply from Kax and she didn't come to the bar. He was worried. He didn't want her to be left out but also hoped that she was okay. He took a stroll past her room and knocked on her door. "Kax, are you in there?"

The door opened and her eyes were red and puffy from crying. "Skyler, what are you doing here?" She sniffed.

Skyler's heart dropped he feared the worst. "I sent you a text the plants were approved and you didn't come to the bar. I was worried about you."

"Come in," she said. She sat down on the center of her bed and hugged her pillow.

Skyler noticed a pile of soiled tissues on the floor. "What s going on?" He sat on the end of her bed. "Did somebody hurt you?"

She shook her head. "No, not recently. It was just that today was the hearing for Kreeve and it was just really emotional going."

Skyler's heart sank. "Oh Kax, why didn't you tell me? I would have gone with you. What happened?"

"It was okay Skyler, I didn't have to go. I just had to know for myself and face him one more time. It was really hard but I had to do it. I hope you understand." Kax hugged her pillow tighter.

Skyler moved closer and gave Kax a hug, "Kax I love and I care about you. I never want to see you hurt. I'm so sorry about this. How did it go anyway?"

Kax picked up her head, "Remember how you told me he was fighting to get his pension and a promotion?"

A look of worry crossed Skyler's face. "Yes, what about that? I didn't get a message from Cane."

"Well, Cane might have been willing to work and negotiate with him but Davis was not. She didn't care what he said, she threw the book at him. So he got a dishonorable discharge and no pension." Kax said, cracking a smile.

"Well I guess she is good for something." Skyler teased.

Kax leaned in and gave Skyler a kiss on the cheek, "Thank you for everything you have done for me, this and the years before. You might not be perfect but you're working on it." She kissed him a bit more.

Skyler pushed her back, "Kax what are you doing?"

The redness in her eyes was fading, "Skyler, you're always there for me. I wanted to repay you."

Skyler stood up off the bed. "Kax, I love you and deeply care for you. I help you because I care and am a good guy. But right now you're going through an emotional roller coaster. Please, please don't take this the wrong way but I think getting some rest is the best for you right now."

She let out a deep sigh and the sadness returned to her eyes, "I'm sorry, I just don't know how to react right now. Even if we don't do it, would you like to stay the night and keep me comfortable?"

Skyler let out a long sigh. He scanned around the room and noticed a small couch. He pulled a flask out of his pocket and handed it to Kax. "Here is something to drink, it helps me when I need to celebrate and when I'm feeling sad. I will stay with you but I'm sleeping on the couch. I'll keep you company and take care of you but that is it. I love you, Kax. I would never take advantage of your vulnerability."

She took the flask from him. Taking a sip, she smiled at him, "You're a good friend, Skyler."

Chapter 32

The end of the school year arrived. The plants were finished and approved. They had spent a few weeks working on getting them ready to be shipped out. Skyler stopped by Michael's room. "So you got your marks in and heading back to Earth?"

Michael picked his head up from his suitcase. "Yup, I did my work and Earth base has been cleaned up so I can take most of the summer off to take care of my father and do any work they want over the computer. I am done here. Sorry to leave you alone for another summer, buddy."

Skyler sighed, "Well I hope I get to see you again one day. When I came out here I applied for a posting. I'm out here until I graduate."

Michael put his shirt into the suitcase. "Wait…you mean to tell me that this may be the last time I see you? If you are staying in the other galaxy and I am going back to Earth. Wow."

Skyler put his hands in his pocket. "For now, but hey, when I become a captain I'll make sure to request you for my crew."

Michael sat down on his bed. "Is it because of your mother? Is that why you're not coming back?"

Skyler let out a deep sigh. "One of the reasons. She isn't going to travel out here just to fight with me. I also don't have anything left for me back on Earth. I can go just about anywhere."

"Well, it's been a nice four years knowing you. But I guess this is what we figured would happen as we got further into our careers." Michael stood up and gave Skyler a pat on his back, "What are you going to do without me?"

Skyler shrugged, "Well, Kax is here until the end of the summer, Perry is here until he graduates, so I got some friends. Me and Kandice have become friends and she's agreed to be my wingman. The gang won't be the same without you."

Michael sighed, "I have gotten used to all of you and for the first time in my life I have friends. I know I will see you all again. This will not be the end."

Skyler gave Michael a hug. "I'll see you around. Until then you go out and be the best you can be."

Epilogue

Cane stepped out on his small transport ship and onto a swampy landscape. He stepped toward the bog, holding a glowing pendant in his hand. The bog waters began to bubble. Cane stood there watching as two large black eyes arose from the bog. They were like two periscopes rising from the water. Cane held out the pendant for them to see. Quickly, the swamp alien the periscope eyes belonged to came out of the water. An alien that resembled a large bipedal salamander approached Cane. "Leon, you return alone?"

Cane bowed his head, "I'm sorry, Lord Ackle, my return is late and alone. Levi passed on many years ago, but I have the crystal and am returning it for the ritual."

Lord Ackle sniffed the air. "Is there another?"

Cane raised an eyebrow. "I came alone, as instructed. What other do you speak of?"

"You smell like a lighter version of Levi. Did he by chance have a son?" Lord Ackle enquired.

Cane understood and nodded his head. "Yes, Levi has one son, Skyler. Why is he important?"

Lord Ackle went over and took the crystal out of Levi's hand, "The son bears the same DNA as his father. Only someone with Levi's DNA can complete the ritual. I will hold onto the crystal until your safe return with the son."

Cane bowed his head one more time. "Thank you, my Lord. I will return with the boy as soon as I can."